DIGGING

A NOVEL

by

LU ANNE STEWART

DIGGING

Published by
Fat Dog Books
California, USA

Cover by Summer Hanford

Fat Dog Books
ISBN: 978-0-9991370-6-2

Literature & Fiction
Printed in the United States of America

Visit our website at www.fatdogbooks.com

ACKNOWLEDGMENTS

This book was inspired and nurtured over many years by a large cast of characters who deserve my heartfelt thanks. I am grateful to my husband, Richard Stewart, a fine journalist who can always be counted on for thoughtful editing and unconditional support. I thank my Aunt Isabelle Dold and my late Uncle Ed for always encouraging me to pursue my love of writing.

I am grateful to the student editors at my college newspaper, the Daily Pennsylvanian, and to my teachers and mentors at Columbia's Graduate School of Journalism for instilling in me a fiery passion for the practice of good journalism and the importance of freedom of the press in our democracy. That fire sparked the idea for Digging.

Special thanks are due to the many friends, writers and readers who reviewed this manuscript at various points in its development and offered invaluable feedback, including Amy Brown, Patricia Averbach, Gerry Wilson, Anna Philpot, Shirley Rush Dean and Joe Baker. I also want to express my gratitude to the amazing writers Connie May Fowler and Ann Hood, who led workshops at the Miami Writers Institute that I had the good fortune to attend. Their guidance and insight changed my writing life and helped make Digging possible.

Finally, I offer my sincere thanks to Fat Dog Books, which gave me the chance to bring this book into the world.

DEDICATION

For Richard, my best editor and supporter,
and for Aunt Isabelle and Uncle Ed, who made my dreams possible.

"Our citizens may be deceived for awhile, and have been deceived; but as long as the presses can be protected, we may trust to them for light."
—Thomas Jefferson

DIGGING

Chapter One

If I tell you right here at the beginning that I came to the sorry little town of West Wicklow, Rhode Island, for a noble cause, to follow my life's calling as a reporter, would that sound overblown? Maybe, in hindsight. But this was the summer of 1977, a time when journalists were heroes, just a year after Robert Redford played one in the movies. And I was 21, spring-loaded with dreams, a journalism degree burning a hole in my pocket. I'd grown up watching reporters exhume buried things. I wanted to dig for a living.

I had no way of knowing then that my byline, Meg Sullivan, would become known beyond the borders of that town, or that such a heavy price would be assessed for unearthing what lay hidden there. Even now, when I'm sometimes asked to speak of these events, certain memories race scatter-shot across the senses. The dull orange glow at the bottom of a winding road. An acrid smell on the wind. The empty monotone of a voice that I would come to discover was lying without shame.

I set out for Rhode Island on a sweltering August morning, driving away from the Philadelphia rowhouse I'd called home, my stoic father waving in the rear-view. I was a human hot air balloon, all of my mooring lines cast off, ready to float northward and fall back to earth in a town I'd never heard of, where I knew not a soul, but where the publisher of a twelve-thousand-circulation daily newspaper had offered me a job.

By the time I reached the West Wicklow exit on I-95 it was early afternoon. The ramp deposited me on a two-lane road where thick stands of pines gradually gave way to tiny Cape Cod homes with worn paint and sagging rooflines, then to double- and triple-decker apartment buildings standing shoulder to shoulder. The winding road led steadily downhill. I remembered that Ruskin, the publisher, had called it "the Valley."

The road made a sweeping turn. Suddenly before me rose up a massive structure, sprawling across the equivalent of several city

11

blocks, built of grey, rough-faced granite, standing some ten stories high. The building's sheer scale and the unrelenting expanse of drab stone made me think for a moment that the sun must have moved behind a cloud.

A tall clock tower sat atop the roof, as if keeping a stern eye on the entire complex, and beneath the clock was chiseled in block letters: *Hampton Mill est. 1859*. Hundreds of white-framed windows marched across the entire facade, one after the other, row upon row. Many of the windows were broken and, at first, I assumed the whole place was abandoned. But then I spotted a handful of cars parked in the lot and small signs in some of the first-floor windows. Auto Repair. Tool & Die. As the road turned again over a small bridge, I saw that the giant mill sat on the bank of a narrow and murky river.

I passed three more of these structures as I made my way into town to find the office of the *Arcadia Valley Daily Times*. The newspaper building was so unassuming that I had to circle the center of town twice before I spied it, clinging to the crest of a small hill on Frontenac Street, one block up from Main. At first, the place looked to be in decent shape, with crisply painted white clapboard along the front entrance and a smart blue-and-white sign with the name of the paper in a flowing script. But as I parked in the lot on the side, I could see that behind the white facade, the rest of the building was a ramshackle series of additions that seemed to tumble down the hillside.

None of this dampened my enthusiasm. When I reached for the front doorknob and entered, I felt the weight of the moment keenly with each step. In that instant, my life as a journalist began.

Clive Ruskin looked completely different from my mental image of him. In our only phone conversation I'd conjured him up as a paunchy cigar-smoker with a comb-over. But instead the man who rose from his desk to shake my hand was tall and reed-like, bending slightly from the waist in an effort to reach down to my level. He had a bearing that felt like New England to me, earnest and reserved, as though stepping out of a Hawthorne novel.

"Good to have you aboard," he said, gesturing to one of two plain wooden chairs positioned in front of his large oak desk. He reached over to hand me a folded newspaper.

"Today's edition. Required reading. You'll start tomorrow. 7 a.m. sharp."

"I'm looking forward to getting to know the town," I said.

An awkward pause. I tried to fill it with the first thing that occurred to me. "What's the story on those huge buildings along the river?"

He leaned toward me, his eyes drilling into mine. "Why? What have you heard?"

I realized I had misstepped somehow. *Why was he so touchy?* I shifted in my seat. "Nothing. I just saw them as I was driving in and was curious."

The ridges across his forehead relaxed. He sat back in his chair. "They're our dinosaurs. Old textile mills from the heyday of New England's manufacturing era. Tablecloths and draperies. Sweaters. Lace of all kinds. And underwear. All made here in the Valley by thousands of workers who filled up those hulking monsters."

His annoyance with my question seemed to evaporate and now he warmed to the task of schooling me in this history, looking off into the distance as he spoke. He explained how the mills were located all along the Arcadia River that wound through the Valley, using hydroelectric power generated by massive turbines turned by the dammed-up water flow.

"When cheaper labor lured the manufacturers south, they started to close, one by one. First Barkin Mill. Then Saunders, Valley, Hampton, Century. A few of them still do some small-scale manufacturing, but most of the jobs have moved away. Now they house cheap commercial rental space for small businesses. They're hanging on." He appeared to catch himself. "Now don't think this is some dying town. Plenty of news here for you to sink your teeth into." He stood up, and I did the same. "7 a.m. sharp. Ask for Bob in the newsroom. He'll show you how to do the cops beat."

Afterward, I took a walk up Main Street. I wanted to get a closer look at this place that Ruskin had made a point to emphasize was not dying. That comment, plus the way he'd barked at my question about the mills, had left me with an unsettled feeling, like walking into a darkened house.

It was easily ten degrees cooler than Philly had been that morning, with a crisp breeze to balance the late afternoon sun. I passed a low-slung, yellow-brick Town Hall with a sign announcing the departments inside: Town Clerk. Tax Assessor. Planning & Zoning. Public Works. Another sign at the far end marked the entrance to the Police Department. Two Crown Vic cruisers sat out front, their shiny black and chrome surfaces blinding in the reflected sunlight. Next door, a sturdily built young man in a khaki uniform washed a rescue wagon in front of the fire station while two other men in khaki sat on the front step conversing. *So far, so good.* Just a normal all-American town.

The men at the firehouse turned out to be the only souls on the street as I continued down Main, passing a Chinese restaurant, then Medeiros Shoe Repair, then a pawn shop. The retail strip grew seedier the further I got from Town Hall. Up ahead in the next block, I could see a neon sign, illuminated despite the fact that it was daylight, with the lettering GIRLS XXX. A pang of queasiness stirred in my stomach. *What am I doing in this increasingly creepy town?* I drew in a deep breath. *Don't be a baby.* Maybe the seedier the better. More troubles equals more news.

I stopped to look at the shop in front of me. A painted sign over the doorway said Mugsy's, with a swirl of steam coming up out of the "u" and diner-style coffee mugs on either side tipped at jaunty angles. Definitely more appealing than the strip club sign. Maybe this was a good place to start mixing with the locals. I ducked inside.

A dull aluminum counter with worn red leatherette swivel stools ran the length of the narrow shop. A few patrons were scattered about. *Finally, fellow humans!* A teenage boy and girl sipped Cokes at a small table near the door. Chatter rippled from a rear booth stuffed with four 50ish women.

Halfway down the counter sat a young man about my age, in a light blue Oxford shirt and jeans, reading the paper. His shaggy brown hair reached almost to his shoulders and he stroked a neatly trimmed beard as he read. As I approached he looked up and gave a nod that I interpreted as a sign of welcome. I sat down a few stools away and ordered coffee.

"You want it regular?" asked the stout man behind the counter.

I nodded. "And with some cream and sugar, please."

His eyes narrowed. "Regular in Rhode Island means with cream and sugar," he said, grabbing a mug from the rack along the wall. "You new in town?"

I felt suddenly conspicuous. "Sure am. Just got a job at the paper."

He harrumphed. "Good." He clanged the spoon against the inside of the mug as he stirred. "They need some fresh blood over there." He set the coffee in front me. "You know," he said in a lower

14

voice, "a lot goes on in this town that never ends up in the paper."
He raised his eyebrows and sauntered away toward the other end of
the counter.

I glanced over and saw the brown-haired guy looking my way. He
looked back at his paper; a few minutes passed.

"They're burning, you know," I heard him say in a matter-of-fact
voice.

I looked over at him. "I'm sorry, what was that?"

He swiveled his stool toward me. "They're burning. The mills."
Then he folded his paper in half, and half again, tucked it under his
arm and rose to leave. "You'll see," he said as he passed me.

When he reached the door, he looked back. I noticed for the first
time how intense his eyes were—a bottomless brown that seemed to
draw me in.

"Good luck," he said with a trace of a smile.

As I drove off to find my new apartment, rented sight-unseen
over the phone, I couldn't stop thinking about what the guy at
Mugsy's had said about the mills. He didn't look like a crackpot—
more like one of those serious grad-school types at mixers back in
college, the ones who never danced. So what was behind the cryptic
comment?

I headed out of town on Main and turned right at Valley Mill, a
more compact version of the others I'd seen but still towering over
the small houses and triple-deckers around it. I passed a teenage girl
holding the hand of a little boy as he wobbled over a broken stretch
of sidewalk. They looked so small in the shadow of the giant mill.

The road rose sharply up a steep grade, twisting along low stone
walls that looked like they'd been there since the Revolution. Finally I
reached the summit and turned into a driveway with a crooked
mailbox bearing the number 302 in a hand-painted scrawl.

I got out and stopped to look at the view. Below me the Valley lay
like a miniature Christmas village, laced with winding roads, rooftops
and church spires, all arranged on a blanket of green. It looked
decidedly more charming than the ground-level views I'd seen so far.
From this vantage point, the river was hidden but I could guess its
route, my gaze following each cluster of houses that led to the tower
of a mill, then a jog in the route and then another cluster, and
another tower, then another. Miles away, beyond the green, where a
swatch of blue shimmered in the haze, the river poured itself into

Narragansett Bay on its way to the sea. With that glimpse of the bay, I felt my spirits lift. Maybe I could grow to love this town.

"Are you Meg?"

I looked back at the split-level house at the end of the drive to see a woman with short, platinum hair poking her head out the front door.

"You must be Francie," I said, walking up to meet her. She was middle-aged but came down the front steps with the quickness and bounce of a teenager, stuffed into denim cut-offs and a Red Sox T-shirt.

She motioned to me to follow her up a stairway on the outside of the house that led to an apartment over the garage. "Nothing fancy, but you'll be comfy here," she said, jiggling the key in the lock until the doorknob turned.

Inside was a tidy apartment encased in caramel-colored wood paneling, with a kitchenette, small oak dining table with two captain's style chairs, and a couch upholstered in a homey pattern of fall foliage. On the wall over the couch hung a small framed painting that could have come from a paint-by-numbers kit: water cascading over a dam as a deer grazed on the bank. It was all corny as hell, and yet it triggered in me an inexplicable wave of happiness. I loved every paneled, homespun inch of it. A place of my own.

"Your bedroom and bath are right through there," Francie said, pointing. "Come downstairs once you get your stuff moved in, and we'll handle the paperwork." She paused. "My only rules are no loud music, no troublemaking. But you look like a nice girl."

That night I sat at my own dining room table for the first time, eating a frozen turkey dinner I'd grabbed at a convenience store along the way and cooked in my miniature oven. On the kitchen counter, Steely Dan played from my 8-track. A new energy coursed through me, a sensation of being fully in charge, with no limits on the choices I could make, or how my life might unfold.

I visualized myself starting the job the next morning. Getting out there and digging information out of people. Comforting the afflicted and afflicting the comfortable. Suddenly the cocky world-is-my-oyster feeling vanished, replaced by a searing, soul-sucking panic. Could I actually do this? All my life, I'd been invariably described as "quiet." I fidgeted when all eyes turned to me to speak. And now, starting at 7 a.m. tomorrow, I was expected to transform myself into a female version of Bob Woodward? Carl Bernstein in a bra? (Or without one, perhaps.) What the hell did I know about being a reporter?

Calm down. Remember your training. I'd spent the last four years at a women's college called Oakmont on the outskirts of Philly, run by an order of feisty, politically progressive Catholic nuns and renowned for its muckraking journalism program. The school attracted a stellar faculty of veteran journalists, and now I thought back to the words of one particular professor, Martin Schramm, a raspy-voiced, retired *New York Times* editor who taught investigative reporting.

"Not everyone is cut out for this work," he said to the class on the first day, striding around the room and glowering down at each of us. "Will it bother you if people think you're rude, or too aggressive, or not polite? Here's a news flash: Investigative journalism is not a polite endeavor! You need to have some..." He paused. "Moxie." He lingered on the word, like slow-rolling tires on gravel.

Ah, yes. Moxie. A quality that didn't come naturally to me. But I was determined to cultivate it; to reshape my personality if that's what it took to excel in this job.

I opened up the paper Ruskin had given me. Across the top was a lead story about the previous night's Zoning Board meeting. Three people had spoken against a neighbor for working on junk cars in his driveway. Along the left side was a column that said "Around the U.S." Elvis' funeral draws 75,000. Details emerge from Son of Sam killer's confession. NASA prepares to launch Voyager 2 probe.

I flipped the paper over to read what was below the fold. There, in the bottom right corner, a headline said:

Fire at Barkin Mill Drives Residents From Nearby Apartment House

Beneath the headline, a black-and-white photograph showed a dark and chaotic scene. One team of firefighters trained hoses on bright flames raging from the mill's second-story, while another group sprayed water on a triple-decker apartment standing just across a narrow street.

In the foreground of the shot stood a cluster of people—an elderly woman in a nightgown, kids with no shoes, a bare-chested man, women holding crying babies. Suddenly I drew in a sharp breath. Standing in the midst of the crowd was the guy from the coffee shop. He was being interviewed by a young reporter holding a notepad. I glanced down at the byline. *By Robert Marchand.* Probably the "Bob in the newsroom" Ruskin mentioned.

17

Quickly I scanned the story. Twelfth mill fire in West Wicklow this year. Residents of low-income housing nearby "living in fear." Fire chief says investigation will continue.

Finally, this passage:

Eric Fields, director of the Alliance for Social Justice (ASJ) West Wicklow chapter, said the problem was larger than last night's fire.

"Mill fires are becoming alarmingly frequent in this community, and the people being victimized don't have the resources to fight back," Fields said, vowing to help area residents bring their concerns to the Town Council at its meeting next week.

I looked again at the faces of the apartment house residents. One young woman stood on the outskirts of the group, staring up at the flames shooting from the mill. Her face was contorted, mouth open, her hands clasped together tightly under her chin. What was her story? These were all people with a story that needed to be told. And the mills themselves—what story lay hiding behind those stone walls? I thought again of Schramm and one of his favorite bits of advice that now rang in my ears. *Be constantly asking yourself: what's wrong with this picture? What doesn't make sense? Maybe there lies a story.*

Chapter Two

I met Bob Marchand in the murky light of dawn outside the newspaper building. We walked together to police headquarters to check the overnight blotter. He had the quick, intense gait of someone who knew what he was doing, and long sandy hair that bounced with each step.

"Ever cover cops before?" he asked.

I felt a flicker of nerves. Didn't want to sound too green.

"A few times. A couple of arrest stories for my college paper back in Philly. Some court hearings."

"So, you know how they can be. A little wary of you at first. You've got to build up some trust. Then they'll start giving you stuff."

He explained he'd joined the *Times* three years ago out of the University of Rhode Island journalism program. According to the paper's custom, the "cops beat" always went to the newest reporter on staff.

"Now I get to hand it off to you. Moving up to cover Town Council and politics. That's the beat I've always wanted." He told me how he'd grown up in the Valley, in a French-Canadian family that had roots going back to the French and Indian War.

"The Valley names will take some getting used to. Most people here are either French or Portuguese descent," he said. "So you'll see Archambault, Boucher, Charbonneau. Then you'll have your Petrarca, Ferreira, Pinheiro. You'll get the hang of the spellings and pronunciation."

Inside, the station was dim and quiet, with band-aid-colored walls and scuffed brown linoleum. A balding uniformed officer sat at a raised countertop with a frosted plastic panel in front.

"How's it goin', Teddy?" Bob called up to him.

"It's goin'," he replied without looking up. Then he spotted me and a frown creased his forehead.

"This is Meg Sullivan—she's going to be doing the blotter now," Bob said quickly. "Meg, Teddy's the desk sergeant. He always knows everything that went on in town from the night before."

Teddy let out a loud laugh that bounced off the walls. "Well, maybe not everything, Bobby."

He slid open a window in the plastic panel and pushed a wire basket filled with paper out onto the counter. "Here's the overnight reports," he said. "Pretty quiet."

"Thanks, Teddy," I said, grabbing the basket and trying to make my voice sound just right. Respectful but strong. Not too girlish. It was the first time in my new professional life that I felt self-consciously female. I probably didn't look much like a hard-nosed reporter to Teddy. Just a wisp of a girl: five-foot-two and rail-thin, with red hair in ringlets around a freckled face. I would need to compensate for my looks with an extra helping of moxie.

I followed Bob into a small room just off the entrance and we sat down at a wooden table to review the reports for anything newsworthy.

"A lot of these you can skim and ignore," he said. "Domestic disputes where nobody's arrested, traffic stops, suspicious person reports where they don't find anything."

Despite that advice, I kept getting drawn into page after page of sad stories. People passed-out drunk, getting evicted, their car breaking down and no money to fix it. Every report was a bad day in somebody's life. But every sad story wasn't news.

"Here's one that's worth including," Bob said, sliding a report over to me with the words "Barkin fire" written in pencil in the top corner. Millicent Viera, 86, one of the residents who had fled her apartment building next to the mill, suffered an apparent heart attack later that night as she waited for Red Cross to find her temporary shelter. A West Wicklow police officer on the scene administered CPR, and she was transported by rescue to Arcadia County Memorial Hospital, where she was pronounced dead.

"Normally a heart attack isn't a story but..." Bob said. I nodded. Poor Millicent. It struck me what a strange thing I was doing, assessing whether someone's death was news.

Together we flagged a half-dozen reports, mostly petty crime— items stolen from a car, a purse snatching—and I took careful notes on each. Afterward, we stopped by the next room up the hall, the Detective Division, to see if they were working on any bigger cases.

Inside, a handful of detectives in plain clothes milled around. Bob introduced me to the head of the division, Lieutenant Armand Pelletier. He looked to be about my dad's age, broad-shouldered and trim, with touches of grey at the temples. He shook my hand.

"Welcome to West Wicklow," he said with a smile. "We'll do our best to make it interesting for you." Then he put his arm around Bob's shoulder. "So, what—you're getting kicked upstairs, Bobby? Us lowly cops are too small time for you now?"

"Funny guy," Bob shot back. "Not sure if covering Town Council is much of an improvement over you guys."

Pelletier and the other detectives laughed. He slapped Bob on the back. "Say hello to your dad for me." Then he gave me a little wave. "See you bright and early tomorrow, miss."

The newsroom clattered like a rickety trolley car at high speed. I sat at my desk in the corner of the giant room and tapped out my police blotter briefs, the clicks of my blue IBM Selectric blending into the keystrokes of the other three reporters, all of us writing furiously to meet the 10 a.m. deadline. The United Press International newswire machine whirred at its own, slightly higher pitch, and floating above the baseline din were ringing phones and intermittent shouts from managing editor Ned Shuster as he reviewed the reporters' copy at his work station in the center of the room.

He was the only one of us with a computer—part of a new technological advance in transforming reporters' stories into print. Bob had explained the process to me that morning. Our typewritten pages were hand-fed into a scanner, which sent them to Shuster's computer screen for editing. The stories then traveled through yet another humming machine that turned the words into long, thin strips of hole-punched paper tape. The M.E. wound up each story-tape as it spooled onto the floor, marked it by name with a green felt pen, secured it with a rubber band and dropped it down a chute to the production room on the floor below. There they would run the tapes back through another machine that spit out columns of type to be pasted onto pages. The pages were photographed and the negatives were burned onto plates for printing.

"Sullivan! Where's the blotter?" Shuster barked. He kept his eyes trained on his monitor. "It doesn't have to be Tolstoy, kid." He stuffed out his cigarette and immediately lit another. He looked like an aging hippie, maybe forty, with oval wire-rimmed glasses and greying hair pulled back in a short ponytail. His rasp reminded me of Schramm's.

"Almost done," I called back. It was my first piece of writing as a professional reporter and I wanted it to be good.

Bob had told me that Shuster was "a real newsman," a former reporter and assistant managing editor at the *Louisville Courier-Journal*, where he won a Pulitzer for an investigative series on slumlords.

"Don't spread this around," Bob had said on the walk back from police headquarters that morning, "but the word is that Ruskin was able to get him cheap because Ned had a drinking problem. They say he's on the wagon now."

I worked on the last item in my police blotter round-up, the story about Millicent. It was my first time writing about someone who died. I tried to think back to my journalism training. Stay objective. Credibility for a journalist is dependent on the reader trusting that the reporter is an "honest broker," sharing only the confirmed facts without bias or emotion. This was harder than I expected.

After I turned in my briefs at 9:55, I kept my ears open for complaints or questions from Shuster. Finally I heard him mutter, "Christ."

I glanced his way. He looked up.

"Tough one. Millicent."

I nodded.

"The only thing wrong is you should have put that story first," he said. "Remember, Sullivan, writing the police blotter is not trivial work. It's the whole goddam human tragedy."

After deadline, I finally had a chance to take a breath. I leaned back in my swivel chair and looked around the newsroom, taking it all in, savoring the feeling of being a real journalist. All of us worked in a large open space—the expanse of the entire second floor except for the walled-off corner that was Ruskin's office. The room had the look of an old college library, with high ceilings and tall windows all around that let light stream in.

The other staff members who had been hunched over their typewriters or cradling a phone at their ear when I'd first walked in were now starting to push back their chairs and exchange some friendly banter.

Bob came over and introduced me around. John Wilkins, at the desk next to me, covered the neighboring town of Cheshire. Maddie

Monteiro, features/weekend reporter, was the daughter of the *Times* receptionist, Rosie, and had started out writing obits as an intern. She was the only other female on the staff. Sports was the domain of veteran Sandy Frazier, who set down his pipe to shake my hand. I met photographer Joel Stevens as he emerged from the darkroom wearing a black, rubbery apron, on his way to drop the latest batch of prints onto the M.E.'s desk.

Once all of the edited stories had been dispatched down the chute, Shuster called the daily meeting of the news staff. Everyone rolled their chairs over toward his desk and I did the same, all of us forming a circle around him. One by one, each of the reporters talked about the stories they planned to cover that afternoon or evening for tomorrow's paper. Some had town council, school board or zoning meetings that night. Bob planned to follow up on a lead that a local businessman planned to run for town council in West Wicklow.

Shuster swiveled his chair toward me. "Whatcha got?"

"I figured I would follow up on the story of the mill fire," I said, trying to cover the nervousness in my voice. "Check in with the state fire marshal's office on the investigation. Try to interview some of those residents in the apartment building next door."

Shuster nodded approvingly. "And see if you can find poor Millicent's family. Let's try to get a photo of her. Check with Rosie downstairs to see if a picture came in with her obit."

He stood and clapped his hands together like the crack of a bat.

"That's it. Hit the streets, ladies and gentlemen. There's no news to be found in the newsroom."

I parked my car on a side street near the Barkin Mill and began to walk toward the burned-out section of the building. The neighborhood was lined with tattered triple-decker apartment buildings painted in hospital greens and muddy beiges, fanning out from the mill in all directions. The asphalt streets radiated waves of heat from the afternoon sun. I reached the side of the mill, its grey stone slabs charred with a smear of black stretching from the street level to the third story. Just behind the mill, perched one level higher up the hill at 203 Lombardi Street, was the apartment house that had been evacuated. The distance between the two buildings was close enough for a child to throw a ball.

In front of the apartment building, a little boy about five rode a tricycle over the cracked sidewalk. He looked up as I approached and broke into a grin, his dark brown eyes framed by thick, curly lashes.

"Watch me go!" he cried, rumbling across the bumpy surface.

"You're fast!" I said. I looked up to the open porch on the second floor. A thin young woman about my age leaned on the rail, her arms folded.

"Be careful, Petey—slow down!" she shouted. He nodded and cut his speed.

"I'm from the newspaper," I called up to her. "Could I talk to you about the fire?"

She arched her eyebrows. "Not sure what good talking will do." Then she turned and leaned against the side of the porch. "But come on up if you want. I ain't stoppin' ya."

I climbed the outside stairway to the porch and she pointed me toward a slouching love seat covered with a flowered bedspread. She kept an eye on the boy below.

"Damn, it's hot," she said. "You want some water or something?"

I said thanks, but I was fine. I pulled my notebook from my bag, introduced myself and learned her name was Darlene Silva. She looked tough and fragile at the same time, her fine brown hair pulled back in a tight ponytail with a doubled-over rubber band.

"So," I asked, "the night of the big fire, what happened to you?"

She pulled a pack of cigarettes from the pocket of her jeans and lit one. Taking a long drag, she craned her neck to check again on Petey. "Remember what I said—don't go past the street." She turned back to me. "Worst night of my life. Nothing much scares me, but I don't mind saying, I was scared shitless."

She stopped herself. "You can't say that in the paper, right? Shitless?"

We both laughed. She reached over and tapped on my notebook where I had just written the word. "Just say scared stiff. That's better."

Gradually she began to tell me about that night. Woken from a sound sleep by a crackling sound, shouting and the smell of smoke. Then sirens. Someone pounding on the door. "Get out! Get out!" Scooping up Petey, sleeping, like deadweight in her arms, her in just a T-shirt and underwear. Racing barefoot down the wooden steps with Petey on her shoulder, and then he wakes up, a soft cry that turns into a shriek. Standing out on the sidewalk with the neighbors, a chaotic jumble of flashing lights, hoses, more sirens. As she told me the details I could feel my own heart thumping. It was hard to stay focused on writing.

Darlene took another puff on her cigarette, then snuffed it out roughly in a metal ashtray on the porch rail. "I heard the fireman say they needed to keep spraying water on the roof and side of our building so the fire wouldn't jump over from the mill. That was great, except it was a hot night and everybody was sleeping with their windows open. I don't have much, but what I did have turned into a wet, stinking mess."

She said the Red Cross was helping her and the other residents get back on their feet. I asked if she knew Millicent. "Yeah, that was a rotten shame," she said, shaking her head. "Nice old woman. Lived alone. I heard she had a son in Florida, but they were having trouble getting in touch with him."

I asked if she planned to come to the town council meeting next week.

"I'll be there," she said firmly. "We all will. Something's wrong. All these mills going up in flames. That guy, Eric, he's the first one to try to help us. Just because we don't have a lot of money doesn't mean they can treat us this way."

Suddenly she looked intently at me. "You went to college, right?"

I nodded, shifting on the lumpy love seat, thrown off by having a question posed to me.

"Well, I was smart in school," she said. "In high school. I made good grades. Then things took a different turn, I guess." She looked away, out toward the mill towering over us. "But what I'm saying is, don't treat us like we don't matter."

I closed my notebook. "Thanks for telling me your story. Maybe it will help." But even as the words left my lips I knew they sounded empty.

"Hey," she said. "I wait tables at the Estrella restaurant on Main. My mom watches Petey, thank God, or I don't know what I'd do. You oughtta stop by sometime. Ever have Portuguese food?"

"No, never, but I'd like to try it."

She smiled and we shook hands. It wasn't hard to picture her in high school, raising her hand, being quick with the answer. I felt unsettled inside, like I was seeing another version of how my life could have turned out. I remembered my dad using the old Irish expression, "There but for the grace of God…"

25

Walking back to my car, I spotted a familiar figure on the opposite side of the street, farther up the steep hill. It was Eric Fields, standing in front of one of the apartment houses, writing something on a clipboard in his hand, then continuing upward. I quickened my pace and caught up to him at the crest of the hill.

I called his name. As he turned around, a slow smile spread across his face. I was going to remind him that we'd talked in the coffee shop but it was clear that he already remembered me.

"Ah, the new Lois Lane of West Wicklow," he said, using his hand as a visor to shield his eyes from the sun's glare.

The attempt at smart-aleck humor surprised me. I thought he was the ultra-serious type. I extended my hand. "Actually, the name is Sullivan—Meg Sullivan. Good to meet you, officially."

He swiped his hands on his jeans before shaking. "Apologies. It's a sweaty day for canvassing."

We started walking side-by-side up the hill. He explained he was knocking on as many doors as possible surrounding the mill to encourage people to come out to the council meeting. I told him about the story I was working on, and that I'd just talked to Darlene.

"Yes, yes, Darlene," he said. "Smart girl. Very strong. She'd do anything to protect that little boy."

"I'd like to talk to more of the residents impacted by the fire," I said. "Could you help me with that?"

"Of course. Glad to see that the *Times* is finally taking more of an interest in this problem." He paused in front of another triple-decker. "This is my next stop." He held the clipboard out in front of me. "Here, copy down a few of these names and addresses. You can probably catch some of them at home."

"Before you go," I said, jotting the information in my notebook quickly, "tell me what you plan to do at the council meeting next week."

His face turned serious. "We'll be trying to get the attention of these council members. This is not just a series of fires. It's pretty clear that these are crimes. And they're not victimless crimes."

I was startled that he used the word "crimes." My heart began to pound. "What makes you certain they're crimes at all?"

"Open your eyes, Meg!" His voice had an urgent edge. "Someone must be benefitting from these fires. And someone—or many someones—are looking the other way."

26

I kept writing furiously to capture his words, but wanted to press with another question. "What evidence do you have for that?"

His eyes locked on mine. "That's for our law enforcement and fire marshals to figure out." He paused. "And, I hope, for determined reporters like yourself." He reached into his pocket and handed me his card. "Good luck with your interviews," he said, turning to climb the steps. "Call anytime."

Walking back down the hill to the first address on my list, I found myself struggling to get a handle on this Eric Fields. Which was he: impassioned crusader, helpful source, borderline flirt? All of the above?

Whatever he was, he'd given me a hell of a quote for tomorrow's story.

Chapter Three

My feature on Darlene and the other fire victims ran above the fold on my second day on the job.

"Pretty damned good for a newbie, Sullivan," Shuster had shouted at me as he edited the story that morning. "One question: What color was the little boy's tricycle?"

His question threw me. What difference did it make? "It was red. Sort of rusted."

"His *rusted red* tricycle!" he boomed, typing the extra description into the story. "Remember, Sullivan, 'specific is terrific.' Details help the reader see and believe the story you're telling."

He was right—his edit made it better. *Mental note: add more details in future.*

Joel, the photographer, stopped by my desk. "That means he really liked it," he said in a low voice. "When he starts wordsmithing like that, it means he thinks it's already good and he wants to make it even better."

I was starting to see Joel as a guide and interpreter in this new foreign country. I guessed he was a few years older than me, tall and lanky, with frizzy hair that shot out in unexpected directions. Garbed in his long darkroom apron, he had a mad scientist vibe about him.

"Hey," he said, "my wife, Sara, is planning to whip up a big batch of chowder on Sunday night. We wondered if you might want to come over?"

I quickly accepted, never so grateful for an invitation. Up to that point, I'd had frozen dinners every night and was wondering how I'd spend all of the off-hours on the weekend, not knowing anybody but the newsroom crew, Eric Fields and my landlady.

"We'll introduce you to all the Rhode Island cuisine," Joel said, heading back to the darkroom and calling over his shoulder. "Quahog chowder, clamcakes and stuffies."

"What's a quahog?"

John at the next desk looked up with a grin. "That's Rhode Islandese for 'really big clam.'"

The rest of that first week, I found myself easing into the rhythm of the job. Check the police blotter at 7 a.m., stop by Detectives on anything that might deserve a separate story. Get back to the newsroom and write it up by 8:30. Then write whatever story I might have worked on the day before, maybe catch a new assignment from the M.E. on some breaking news that morning, and type everything up by 10. When it was time to head out for lunch, we'd pass the cavernous production room downstairs and see that day's paper rolling off the press.

I was quickly getting to know my co-workers. The circumstances were ripe for becoming close. All of us thrown together in the newsroom, working long hours against tight deadlines, a rag-tag army sharing the same foxhole.

John, who sat almost at my elbow at the next desk, had a sharp wit and a professorial way of stroking his goatee as he spoke. He had majored in English Literature and thought about teaching, but then fell into the job at the *Times* and found his niche. A passionate fan of James Joyce, he would try to sneak snippets of Joycean stream-of-consciousness technique into his stories. Ned would relentlessly edit them out.

Bob was the big brother of the newsroom. Seemed to know everybody in town, where to get a bike repaired, where to find the best Mexican food (a hole-in-the-wall on the Cheshire/West Wicklow line). Everyone called him "The Future Mayor of West Wicklow" but Bob had his career path already mapped.

"After a couple of years here, I'd like to get a job at the *Providence Journal* and then eventually work my way up to editor," he said one day while we were all having lunch at Regina's, the drab but convenient diner next door to the paper.

He was from a big family—five brothers and sisters—and talked about someday having a house full of kids.

"You do realize that this plan requires you to find a girl first," John said.

"Let me get Sara working on that," interjected Joel. He was struggling with a fried fish sandwich, the fish trying to escape the bun at both ends. "She's an obsessive matchmaker. Fixed up the entire newsroom at the last place I worked."

Joel, in addition to being slightly older than the rest of us, was the only one who was married. I'd noticed he was quick to offer advice on any topic.

"Just wait until you cover your first fire with Joel," John said to me. "His job is to tell the firemen where to point the hoses."

Maddie covered events and feature stories on the weekends and had a different schedule than the rest of us. I had my first chance to talk with her late one afternoon that week. Both of us had time to kill before heading out to cover nighttime meetings and she suggested we grab some coffee at Mugsy's.

"So nice to have another girl on the staff," she said, sipping demurely from her mug. She was striking. Long, sleek black hair and dark eyes that danced when she talked. She had just turned nineteen and was working her way through the local community college, still living at home. "Eventually I'd like to get my bachelor's in journalism at URI, where Bob went," she said. "But..." Her voice trailed off, her lips pursed.

"So, is something stopping you?"

She crossed her arms on the table and leaned toward me. "My parents came over from the Azores when they were teenagers, just married," she explained. "They keep to the old ways. Very, very conservative. They let me do the internship at the paper because mom works there. But they never dreamed I would stay and become an actual reporter. You should hear my father: 'What do I say when people ask me what my daughter does? Is she a nurse? Is she a teacher? No, she runs around all hours of the day and night, going up to strangers, asking them questions and taking their picture!'"

I had to laugh. "I guess when you put it that way, it does sound a little weird."

"Don't get me wrong. I love my parents. I just need to work on them to loosen up the leash a little. Believe me, I told them all about you. How you moved up here on your own. Live in an apartment by yourself. I might as well have told them you were from Mars. But you are my proof that there are such things as female reporters."

At the end of that first week, I received my initiation into an important newsroom ritual. Every Friday after work, any members of the staff who were free gathered at The Rockin' Pub, a small bar near the paper. "The Rock," as they called it, had few charms. It was narrow and dim, with a distinctive smell of stale beer mixed with an ammonia-based floor cleaner. A long bar ran along one side and a half-dozen spindly wooden tables were scattered around the room, carved with the initials of lovers past. There was no live music, but they played a defiant, experimental brand of rock on their sound system and played it loud. Old Bowie from his glitter days. Queen. And the new darlings, Talking Heads, just out with a maniacal debut album that, as I look back, formed the perfect soundtrack for the helter skelter of my life at this time.

Psycho Killer was blasting when I walked in with Bob that first night. Joel and John sat at a table in the corner and already had their beers. They were both eating some kind of stuffed appetizer out of a clam shell. I sat down with them and Bob offered to grab beers for both of us from the bar.

"We need to order more stuffies so Meg can get the complete Rock experience," John called after him.

"Ah, another new word to add to my West Wicklow vocabulary," I said.

John leaned in, speaking solemnly. "In addition to the excellent quality and volume of the music, the only other thing notable about The Rock is its stuffed clam, or, in Rhode Islandese, stuffie. In the illustrious tradition of the best bar food, it begins its life frozen and is heated in a microwave by Steve over there, the bartender."

He then reached out to grasp an oversized bottle of hot sauce in the middle of the table. "This is the secret. Shake enough of this on them and they miraculously become good."

Joel chimed in. "You'll get a better quality stuffie when you come over to our place Sunday. The ones here are purely for medicinal purposes. To help us drink more beer."

Bob returned with a tray of stuffies and I took one. John slid the big bottle in front of me. I sprinkled a few drops over it and tried a bite.

"Not bad," I said. "Needs more hot sauce."

They all roared.

"Now she's officially one of us," Bob said.

We talked about the job. Maddie wasn't here because it was her turn that night to work with Ned to put together Saturday's paper. They explained that each of the reporters took turns covering the Friday night shift. Luckily, the paper didn't publish on Sunday, so except for Maddie, the rest of us had weekends off.

"Too bad for Ned," I said. "I guess he can never join us here because he works every Friday night."

They all looked uncomfortable.

"Ah, right," I murmured. I felt stupid for not remembering what Bob had told me.

"Not his kind of place," Joel said gently. "But he hangs out with us sometimes. Parties, that kind of thing. He's a good guy. Not all formal like a boss."

"So, how are things going on your beats, Meg?" John asked. "You've got the West Wicklow zoning board and school district, right?"

"Right, those two in addition to cops and fire."

"God, I dread covering zoning and schools in Cheshire," he said with a dramatic sigh. "They are among the most boring public meetings you will ever sit through. And they always run long into the night."

I nodded. "Had my first zoning meeting last night. Twelve people testified about feral cats running wild in the neighborhood. They blamed a woman on their street for putting out food for them. Got out of there at 11:45 p.m."

"Can't wait to read what you did with that one," said John. "I smell a Pulitzer."

"Go ahead and laugh," said Joel, "but I think Ned is planning to play that one up for Saturday's paper. He sent me out this morning to grab a shot of the cats. Found a few of them behind a dumpster. Mean sons of bitches…"

Suddenly Bob interrupted. "Hey, you know about split shifts, right?" he asked, looking at me. "If you're going to cover a meeting that night, you can take off in the afternoon to compensate."

"Oh, nobody told me," I said. I had worked all day plus two nights that week.

"Ruskin. He'd work us all to death if he could," said John.

"Ah, the old man's not so bad," said Bob.

I asked about Ruskin's background, how he had ended up as a newspaper publisher.

"The thing you have to understand about Ruskin is that he's not a newsman, per se," said Bob. "He has more of a businessman's mind-set. The paper has been in his family forever. The way I heard it, his father was more of a hands-on journalist, covering stories and constantly working all of his sources around town. But he sent Clive off to business school so he could learn the money side and maybe expand the circulation and advertising revenue. Clive took over as publisher about 20 years ago."

John sniffed and sat back in his chair, arms folded. "Well, I've been here three years now and as far as I can tell, the paper has pretty much the same circulation and the same number of pages as it had when I started."

Joel said he thought Ruskin liked the idea of owning a newspaper but didn't have a deep passion about the field of journalism itself. "He enjoys having the position of publisher. It's his identity in the town. He likes writing editorials, but I have yet to read anything remotely controversial in them. He's skittish about offending advertisers."

"I would agree with that," Bob said. "Journalism is not in his gut. Not the same as us."

I thought back to my observations of Ruskin during that first week. Right after deadline each day, he sat at a desk in the far corner of the newsroom, next to a window, tapping at his typewriter. I'd come to learn that this was the time when he would write his editorial or column for the next day's edition. Sometimes he would talk to himself as he wrote, as if urging himself on. "That's the ticket," he would say, or "exactly, that's exactly the point!"

He had written an editorial on the day my fire victims story ran. My professors at Oakmont would have called it an "on the other hand" editorial. It called for compassion for the suffering of those impacted by the fires and saluted the local Red Cross for aiding them, but "on the other hand" cautioned that no official cause had yet been determined for any of the mill fires and that "only time will tell whether this cluster of events will turn out to be a strange and random coincidence or something more."

Now, as I sat around the table at The Rock with my new workmates, I began to understand a little more about where Ruskin fit into this odd puzzle of a town. But there was something I still didn't know. What role might he play in this loose thread of a story I'd begun to pull?

On my first free Saturday, I got into my car and just drove, not worrying about where I was or where I'd end up. The weather had turned much cooler the night before, and I opened the window to let the crisp air rush across my face. It felt good to settle in behind the wheel of the trusty Hornet—a sharp little American Motors sedan, indigo blue, a surprise sixteenth birthday present from Dad. Even more beloved now, a fragment of home in a strange land.

As I drove the streets of West Wicklow and continued on through the winding country roads of Cheshire, the river appeared and reappeared at almost every turn. I would start to feel a little lost and then, suddenly, there was another wooden bridge with the Arcadia flowing under it, at times frothy and swift-moving, other times brown, lifeless. And with each reappearance of the river came another mill—some made of brick, some of stone, some of wooden clapboards. Each time a new mill loomed up before me I felt an uneasy flinch in my gut, like that moment in a horror movie when the suspicious neighbor first appears. I thought again of Darlene's terror that dark night. Finding out what, or who, was setting these old relics ablaze was now my mission.

That evening I stopped at the liquor store near my apartment and bought a bottle of my favorite wine, Rosé d'Anjou, to take to Joel and Sara's on Sunday. In truth, it was the only wine I knew—served in tiny plastic glasses at a college reception I attended once. I hoped it would go with quahogs, whatever the hell they were.

On my way home I passed a Methodist church. Several people walked toward the entrance to a meeting hall on the side of the building. Each of them walked alone. A middle-aged woman. From the other direction, a young man. And walking quickly along a side street was Ned.

As he went inside, I recalled an evening long ago: dad dropping off my Uncle Rory at a hall like that, and me in the back seat, watching him walk in alone.

"Going to these meetings helps him hold onto the good person that we know he is, inside. It takes someone very brave to do what he's doing, Meg," Dad said, his eyes sad in the rear-view mirror.

Very brave, indeed.

"I love rosé—how did you know?" said Sara, greeting me at the door the next night. She had a gentle voice and kind eyes that immediately made me feel at home.

"Come have some snacks while we wait for the chowder to finish cooking," she said, guiding me into the living room. It was a first floor apartment in an old Victorian with a huge bay window in the front. A cool breeze blew through the screens, swaying the sheer white curtains in a lazy dance. From the stereo on one side of the room, Linda Ronstadt lamented a lost love, and, beneath the music, a low, intermittent crackling sound burst from a police scanner on the nearby kitchen counter.

Just then Joel came in and saw me looking at it. "Bet you want one too, huh?" he said, grinning.

"I don't know if I'm that dedicated."

Sara rolled her eyes. "Joel wanted to be a fireman when he was a little boy, so now he gets to chase fire trucks and get paid for it."

"Paid, yes, but not much," he added.

When dinner was ready, we sat around the small table in the kitchen. I learned that Rhode Island style clam chowder was made with a clear broth and chopped-up bits of clam, potato, onion and celery—no cream, no tomatoes. And the only kind of clams to use were the fist-sized quahogs raked from Narragansett Bay by local "quahoggers" (another new word). Everything on the table was delicious but decidedly different from the food I knew. Clamcakes were similar to a fritter or hushpuppy, but with chopped pieces of clam embedded. Sara's stuffies (infinitely better than The Rock's) were worlds away from the deviled clams I ate as a child at the Jersey shore with Dad—these Rhode Island versions had a chunkier stuffing and paprika sprinkled on top. I was only five hours by car from home, yet it was becoming clear this place was in an orbit all its own, where everything from the family names to the food veered off on its own distinct path. For a moment, I saw myself as a traveler in an exotic land, surrounded by things strange and tantalizing.

"Rhode Island seems to have its own way of doing things," I said to my hosts as I loaded my spoon with another mouthful of chowder.

Sara nodded. "We're both from New Hampshire, so we had to learn all of the local quirks," she said. They explained how Joel had been shooting for a small weekly near Manchester and jumped at the chance to become a full-time staff photographer at a daily newspaper. Sara, just out of nursing school, was able to land a job at the county hospital in neighboring Wicklow. They'd been here two years.

"So," I asked, "what's it like living in West Wicklow?"

They exchanged quick glances.

"It's...different," Joel answered. "Hard to describe. Your basic everyday people are great, like anywhere. But the politicians and people in town government..." His voice trailed off for a moment. "I guess the word I would use is 'cagey.' Like when you're talking to someone and you get the feeling they're being careful about what they say."

"But on a brighter note," Sara interjected with a comforting smile, patting my arm, "there's water everywhere—bays, coves, lakes, streams—and we're only about a half-hour from the ocean."

Suddenly, a different sound came from the scanner. A woman's emotionless voice:

"10-10 in progress at Century Mill, 627 Barton Street. Fully involved. Request mutual aid, all stations."

Joel bolted out of his chair, lunging for the camera bag sitting on the floor by the door.

Sara ran to the bedroom and came back with my purse.

"I didn't bring my notebook," I said, flustered.

"I've got an extra," Joel yelled back over his shoulder as he raced out the door.

We jumped into his old Maverick—bright yellow with a black hood and racing stripe along the side; looked like it would get us there fast. He threw it in gear and we roared off, down the winding road to the mill, my body pressed hard against the door on the long, sweeping curve by the cemetery, then jerking back to the left and again to the right as I clung to a hand-hold on the door.

I glanced at Joel. "Does 'fully involved' mean what I think it does?"

He nodded, his jaw muscles tensed.

My thoughts kept pace with the car. I wondered what the scene would be like. Was I up to this? The danger? I'd never covered a fire. Then I realized that coursing through my doubts was a strong current of excitement, and for that, in my very Catholic way, I felt guilty.

Joel seemed to sense my apprehension. "Remember, first of all, be safe. Don't get in the way. Look for the guy in the white fireman's helmet. He'll be the battalion chief in charge."

As we swept around the last curve, the sky turned from indigo to a sallow haze, and then the mill came into view like a giant lantern gone awry, flames shooting out of every opening.

Joel parked and we ran toward the fire. He started shooting, heading toward a group of firefighters as they aimed a hose at the intense wall of flames near the front entrance. At each end of the building, trucks with their ladders extended sprayed strong currents of water at the blaze, with little impact.

37

I ran past a cluster of neighbors watching from the sidewalk opposite the mill. Towers of black smoke rose from the roof. I tried to keep myself from choking with each breath. In the distance, sirens wailed, promising more fire trucks on their way.

I spotted the guy in the white helmet. He stood on the sidewalk next to a white station wagon emblazoned with the department insignia, a large man, his coat bearing the ash and grime of fires past. A name tag said "Chief Nunes." He barked orders to a crew on where to position another hose. When they moved on, I approached.

"Chief..." I began.

His eyes darted my way, impatience flickering. "You're new," he said in a flat voice.

"Yes, sir," I stammered and quickly introduced myself. "What's the current situation as you fight this fire?"

"We've got pumpers and a couple of smaller aerial trucks on the scene now from our department and Cheshire," he said. "Wicklow is enroute with their longest aerial—that'll help us get more water on the upper stories. Luckily, this is one of the vacant mills, no businesses operating in there anymore. And no other buildings too close by—not like what we faced at Barkin."

I asked how the structure became engulfed so quickly.

"Do you know anything at all about these old mills?" he asked, his tone laced with irritation. "Every wooden beam is soaked with a hundred years' worth of oil that they used to lubricate the textile machines. With one spark, they go off like a firecracker."

I jotted notes quickly, trying to capture his words and get another question in. "Any idea at this point on the cause?"

"That'll be a question for the fire marshal," he snapped. And with that, the Wicklow truck pulled up and he strode away to direct the crew.

Once the massive aerial truck stretched out its ladder and began spraying a heavy stream of water over the rooftop, the battle began to turn. Soon I saw Joel coming toward me, his face glistening with sweat.

"See the smoke now?" he said, pointing up. The black plumes had turned to white. "That's a sign they're starting to get control of this thing."

I was impressed. "How'd you learn so much about firefighting?"

He shook his head. "I'm just a crazy fire nut."

I started to take what felt like my first deep breath in an hour. I figured I'd head over to the crowd of onlookers and get a few more quotes.

Suddenly, there was a commotion near the front entrance where a team of firefighters had started to enter the building. Muffled sounds of men shouting, urgent sounds. Outside, the heads of other firemen looking up, turning.

A firefighter appeared in the doorway.

"There's somebody in here!"

Chapter Four

I watched the paramedics carry out the stretcher. The telltale signs: no running or shouting, no IV bag connected. Just an orange blanket covering a human shape from head to toe. The careful tipping downward as they descended the stone steps. The somber loading into the rescue truck.

I found Chief Nunes and learned that the man pronounced dead inside the mill was a vagrant, middle-aged. There were signs he had been sleeping there. An empty quart of beer. A charred wrapper from a pack of cheese crackers. Firefighters searched for any other people inside but found no one.

For a moment, those small details about the dead man's hidden life overcame me and I feared I might cry. But I visualized gathering every drop of emotion tightly into my core, squeezing it dry. I steadied my voice and asked the chief where the investigation would go from here.

"I don't want to jump ahead of the fire marshal's probe," he said. "But obviously, one theory that will need to be looked at is whether this subject was involved in setting this fire, and maybe the others also. If that's the case, a lot of people living near these mills may be able to sleep a little easier."

I was taken aback, surprised that he would throw that theory out there so quickly. And why call this man a "subject"? What about "victim"?

"Did you find any evidence that would point toward this man setting the fire?" I asked.

He stared at me. "Not at this time." His voice was a flat monotone. I got the distinct impression that our interview was over. He turned and walked away.

I started to look for Joel, but instead ran straight into Eric Fields. "Just heard this was happening," he said, breathing hard like he'd been running. He paused. "A man died?"

I nodded. The muscles in his face twitched and he slumped down to sit on the curb. I took a seat beside him.

41

"Did they give you a name?" he asked.

"Not yet."

He sat with his elbows on his knees, hands pressed against his head. "I know some of these guys."

He told me there were about a dozen men, some destitute with no place to live, some unbalanced, some hooked on alcohol or drugs. They had begun taking shelter in the mills each night. Some in groups of two or three. Most chose to fly solo, fearful of being robbed in their sleep, or worse.

"I've been trying to convince them it's too dangerous to stay there. I was working on finding another place."

"The chief said it's possible that this man set the fire here, and maybe the others, too," I said.

Disgust spread across his face. "That sounds like a red herring to me. Why would these guys set fire to the only places in town where they can find shelter?"

I told him I wanted to interview some of the men. "Can you help me find them?"

He nodded. "We can start tomorrow. Early evening. That's the best time."

That night, I woke up at two in the morning. Eyes open in the darkness, I could not erase the image of the blanketed figure on the stretcher. Couldn't sweep away the sadness of those random items he'd left behind in the mill, like the contents of a dead man's pocket. I knew why his death had shaken me so. A year earlier, as a project for Schramm's class, I had mustered the courage to interview a man who slept every night on top of the steam grate on the sidewalk outside my dorm.

John Harrington. That cold morning I approached him was still so vivid in my mind. The blanket that usually covered his head had slumped to his shoulders, his face tilted up to watch a mockingbird singing at the top of a thin young maple planted in the sidewalk. What surprised me were his blue eyes, not the vacant stare of a madman or drunk, but eyes with a trace of light, like an opening in a fence, offering a glimpse inside.

I learned that he'd served in Vietnam in the sixties. He had trouble with his nerves when he returned home, couldn't keep a job. His story became part of an investigative series for the student newspaper on how the social service network was failing vets. In searching public records for the series, I found that John had a sister in Williamsport, Pa. When she came to that spot on the sidewalk and convinced him to leave with her, I was there, snapping a photo.

Now in the middle of this black night, I thought again of the man who died in the fire, and the other men taking shelter in the mills, each of them with a history, family, some failures, perhaps an unfortunate twist of fate. They were not invisible. Not insignificant. And certainly not fair game for scapegoating.

The next morning in the newsroom, Ruskin stopped by my desk as I was writing the fire story. He'd heard on the local AM radio news that morning about the man who died, identified as Conrad Baines, of no permanent address.

"So," he said, "sounds like this may have been our firebug. That's our big headline for today!"

Out of the corner of my eye I could see Ned look up. Later I would realize this was one of those moments that would test me if I was committed to doing this work; that there would be times when it would all boil down to me to state what was objectively true, based on the evidence, or lack thereof. Not just what so-and-so said, or some theory someone spouted, but what could be verified and confirmed. I flipped through my notebook to the Nunes quotes.

"Well," I began slowly, "here in my notes, when I pressed him, Chief Nunes admitted there was no evidence tying this victim to setting this fire or any of the others."

Ruskin grimaced. "Let's just make sure we do a good job with this story," he said. "It's important to the town."

As Ruskin walked back to his office, Ned looked over at me, a small crease of a smile showing, then took another drag of his cigarette. When the paper rolled off the press later that morning, the headline Ned had placed on the lead story, running across all six columns, was this:

13th Mill Fire Claims Life of Local Man
The kicker underneath in smaller type said:
Cause still undetermined; pressure mounts from residents to find answers.

At the reporters' meeting after deadline, I told Ned about my plan to interview other men sleeping in the mills, with some help from Eric as a sort of ambassador.

"I like that approach," he said. "And while you're at it, let's have you work on a longer profile piece on Eric Fields. Man-in-the-news type of thing. Turn it in Friday, and I'll run it as a sidebar with Bob's story on the council meeting protest Thursday night."

I met Eric as twilight settled into the corners of the grey, gothic Knight Mill on Center Street, on the fringe of downtown. This one looked like it belonged in a medieval landscape, fashioned of river rock, with two stone turrets towering high over our heads. As we walked toward a side entrance, I felt the massive weight of the building press in on me. This was the closest I'd been to one of the mills. In the distance I heard the sound of water falling, falling. Peering through the murky light, I could make out the dam where white water rushed to the river below.

We entered through a wooden door with a broken lock, and walked down a long corridor. I pulled my flannel shirt tighter around me. The evenings had grown progressively cooler and a bone-chilling dampness permeated the place.

Up ahead, the hall opened up into a large room. A soft glow lit up the corner where three men sat around an old camping lantern.

"It's Eric," he called out to them. "I've brought a friend."

The oldest of the three raised his hand, beckoning us. In the shadowy light, I could see his face was leathered, stretched over bony features. A ripped maroon parka hung over his shoulders. To his left sat a younger man, mid-twenties, in a thin Valvoline T-shirt. He kept his eyes down, tapping his foot and running his fingers repeatedly through long, stringy brown hair. The third man lay with his back to us and never looked around.

We sat down cross-legged on the ground next to them.

"How are you getting along, Marty?" Eric asked the old man.

"I've got a roof over my head for the night," he replied, his words coming out like the labored ticking of an old clock. "And I've got this light. Not sure where I got it."

Eric smiled. I guessed the lantern might have come from him.

He introduced me. "Meg is writing a story about the mill fires."

"We all heard about Connie," Marty said, suddenly agitated. "That was a damn shame. He never hurt nobody."

Eric tried to soothe him. "I know. He was a good guy. I'd like to get all you guys out of the mills. It's not safe."

"Not safe!" shouted the young man, and then fell silent again.

I asked Marty if he knew anything about the fires.

"All of us guys stay on the move. A night here, then find a new spot the next night." He laughed. "We're a regular traveling circus!" His face grew serious again and he looked intently at me. "I think it's all that garbage they're bringing in. That's what's catching fire."

It was the first comment from him that sounded odd. Was he in his right mind? I asked what he meant.

"I was at Barkin the night before that one went up. I had a good hidey hole there, let me tell you. Tucked into a little cave in the wall. They never knew I was there."

"Who didn't know?"

"The guys on the forklift."

I could see Eric glance my way but I kept my eyes locked on Marty.

"All day long, boxes on boxes came in on pallets stacked up to the ceiling," he continued. Later, after the men left, he got curious and went to look inside one of the boxes.

"I wasn't going to steal nothing," he said, his eyes wide. "Just curious, is all. And so I pried open one of them boxes, and inside was nothing but junk. Old papers, piles of used clothes, scraps of broken furniture. A bunch of crap sealed up in a box."

The lantern light flickered in Marty's eyes as he leaned in toward us, his voice low.

"Sounds like I'm crazy, don't it?"

Chapter Five

As we left the mill, a light rain began to fall. We agreed to meet at an all-night diner called Pokey's on the road headed out of town toward Cheshire. I followed Eric's beat-up Jeep along the twisting road as the rain fell harder, my headlights illuminating the strip of duct tape clinging to his rear bumper. Finally, the diner's neon sign appeared in the mist.

Inside, the place was nearly empty and we slid into a booth in the back. Pokey's had the classic American diner look, bathed in stainless steel with red vinyl upholstery on the barstools and the booth seats, and a small jukebox at the end of each table.

After the waitress took our order and left us alone again, Eric leaned in toward me.

"What do you think?"

I shook my head.

"Not sure what to think. I probably can't quote Marty as any kind of credible source."

"But he's not a nut. I can vouch for him."

"It's okay. What he said is valuable, but I just can't use it yet. I need to find out what's really going on here. What he said about the boxes gives me a place to start digging."

I told him I wanted to visit some other mills to interview more of the men, find out if they remembered anything about what was stored there.

"Whatever you need," he said. "I want to help." The intensity in his eyes caught me for a moment, locked on. For that instant, I felt like we were joined in a cause, and then I pulled myself back. He was my source. Stay objective.

The waitress returned with our coffees. I reached in my bag and pulled out my notebook and pen.

Eric drummed his fingers on the table. "Ah, that's right, we're not just here to eat, are we?"

He'd agreed to let me interview him here for the man-in-the-news profile. "Appreciate you taking the time to do this," I said, flipping to the first blank page in my book.

He tensed slightly, shifting in his seat.

"I'm not so good at talking about myself, actually." He ran his fingers through his shaggy hair, a few strands across his forehead still wet from dashing through the rain. It was the first time I'd seen him look anything other than confident.

I smiled. "It's easy. I can ask you anything, and you have to answer."

He began to laugh, crumpling over to bury his face in his hands, then straightened up and took a deep breath.

"I'm totally at your mercy, ah, I mean your disposal."

I started out with the easy questions: where he grew up, where he went to school. I was surprised to learn that he got his bachelor's at the University of Pennsylvania in my hometown of Philly. As he continued to fill in details, my brain raced ahead. Penn was part of the Ivy League. And he said he grew up on Long Island. I thought again about the duct tape on the bumper of his old Jeep, and everything I'd observed to this point about the issues he cared about and the work he had chosen.

"So, when you were at Penn, was there something that made you decide to pursue this particular kind of career?"

A slight smile crossed his lips. "Perceptive question. Yes, there was a trigger for me. A point that changed my path."

His father was a senior partner at one of the big accounting firms and Eric thought he might want to do something similar in business or finance. He was thinking about getting his MBA, or maybe going to law school.

"In senior year, I volunteered with a group called the Campus Consumer Coalition," he said. "To be honest, it wasn't because I was on a noble mission to help consumers. I heard it was a good activity to have on your grad school application."

He paused as the waitress arrived with bacon and eggs and we made room for the platters on the small table, then continued his story.

His work at the consumer group involved helping residents of the poor West Philadelphia neighborhood that encircled the Penn campus. Evictions. Utility shutoffs. Price-gouging scams. The student volunteers served as advocates and go-betweens, guided by attorneys who worked pro bono.

"I'm ashamed to say I never realized until meeting these people what a bubble I'd been living in all my life," Eric said. His voice had a colorless quality, as if he were describing someone else's memories. "The house I grew up in. The cars. Sailboats and yacht club racing on weekends. Vacations to Europe. So much…" His voice trailed off. I stopped taking notes for a moment and just listened.

"It's not that I think wealth is wrong. My parents worked hard. But I started to realize that I was happier when I was working with people from the neighborhood than I was in my old world."

"So how did you end up in Rhode Island?" I asked.

He explained that his parents offered to pay all his expenses to continue on for a master's or law degree. "But I wanted to start working, earning my own way. And then I heard through contacts at the consumer group that the Alliance for Social Justice was looking for a community organizer in Rhode Island. I started a year ago."

I had to smile, thinking how similar our paths were in that way. Rhode Island reaching out to both of us, drawing us here.

"What, did I say something funny?" he asked.

I shook my head. "No, sorry. I was just remembering how I ended up here. A call out of the blue. I'd never been to Rhode Island, so I had to get out my map of the U.S."

He chuckled. "Well, I was only slightly more familiar than you. The only places I'd visited here were ports that you could sail into. Block Island. Watch Hill. Newport. Very different from life here in West Wicklow."

I pictured Eric as a teenager with his family, sailing into a glamorous harbor with canvas billowing. There was something about sailboats. I'd always been mesmerized by them when Dad and I spent vacations at the Jersey shore. Little triangles of white on the horizon against the vast blue, looking like they might sail off the edge of the world.

"So, you're a sailor, then?" I wanted to hear more.

"That's the one piece of my old life that I held onto. My first week here I was driving along and saw a small boat sitting on a front lawn with a 'For Sale' sign. Just a little daysailer, fourteen-footer, and a total wreck but the price was right for someone of my limited means. I've been fixing her up."

He talked about exploring Narragansett Bay in the tiny sloop, launching it at the ramp in Wicklow Harbor and heading off in no particular direction, letting the wind decide.

"Out there, in a fresh breeze, my head seems to clear. Any problems I left on shore become manageable." He paused. "You ought to try it sometime."

Just then, our waitress returned to clear the table, scooping up platters and silverware into her arms with a clattering that reverberated through the near-empty diner. We both ordered more coffee and she gave me a wink as she turned to leave. She probably didn't know what to make of us. Me with my notebook and pen, scribbling down everything this man said.

We talked for almost another hour as the rain steadily intensified, pelting against the window at our table. He described his work at the ASJ. As he spoke about the people he tried to help, he became increasingly animated, leaning in toward me with his elbows on the table, his hand gesturing in a chopping motion, emphasizing their struggles.

"They're trying to survive the basic challenges of living day to day. Not enough money to pay the rent, buy food, keep the lights on, go to the doctor. We try to link them to agencies, nonprofits, church groups that can help, but also push elected officials for better policies to give them a shot at a good life."

"Is the local government here responding?" I asked.

He smiled. "I think they see us as a nuisance, reminding them of people they would rather pretend don't exist. In a way, it's all part of the history of this town. Decades ago, jobs in the mills were plentiful. You could have a high school education—or not even finish high school—and still get a decent-paying job and raise a family. Then the textile companies in the mills left town. Most people eventually found another way to make a living, their kids went to college and moved up from working class to middle class. But there's this core of people who are the legacy of those mill closings, the ones whose grandparents and parents lost their jobs and their families got stuck in a rut of poverty they couldn't climb out of."

I continued writing with my head down, wanting to capture all he'd said. When I looked up, he was peering at the songs listed on the tabletop jukebox.

"You know we've been in here this whole time and nobody has played a single song," he said.

I looked around. There were only two other patrons, an old man in a booth at the back and a middle-aged guy with a tool belt sitting at the counter.

"Somehow, this doesn't seem like a music kind of crowd."

His eyes, which had looked so serious and earnest a few minutes ago when he was talking about his work, now took on a different glint.

"Well, I think it's just much too quiet in here," he said, reaching into his pocket and digging out a quarter.

"So," he continued, "we have to find a song we can agree on."

He turned the dial to flip from one page of songs to another. Most of them were from the generation just before ours, 1950s-era oldies.

"Elvis fan?" he asked.

"Not...really..."

"Nope, me neither."

The parade of hits from Fats Domino, Bill Haley and the Comets and Little Richard continued. Eric looked frustrated.

"C'mon. There's got to be something at least from the '60s."

Finally, he turned the last page. Simultaneously we both said, "hey!"

He looked at me. "Ronettes?"

"Used to dance to that one when I was nine," I said.

"Classic Motown. Nothing better." He slid the quarter into the slot and pushed the worn plastic buttons for E17.

The opening drum blast of "Be My Baby" rocked the diner. *BUM. Pa-Bum. Boom! BUM. Pa-Bum. Boom!*

We listened as the vocal track began, Eric slapping his hand on the Formica table with every beat. Me, hovering halfway between enjoying it and feeling awkward. The tool belt man glanced over his shoulder and gave us a thumbs-up.

As the song played, I had the strange sensation that everything about this moment was more vivid than everyday life. In a vaguely unsettling way. The sounds louder, the stainless steel of the diner walls shinier. Eric, sitting across from me. The man in the news.

When I pulled in the driveway close to midnight, Francie's light glowed in the front window. It was always on when I returned late from covering meetings. Nice to know somebody was looking out for me so far from home.

In the handful of conversations we'd had so far, I learned that my landlady was an avid outdoorswoman raised in the mountains of Maine. That explained the pair of snowshoes nailed to the side of her house, remnants of life in deep snow country. "I still miss seeing snow on the ground all winter," she'd told me, her eyes wistful. "All we get here is freezing rain and slush, maybe the occasional Nor'easter with a puny six inches to shovel."

She'd followed a guy to Rhode Island in her twenties, married him and settled here, getting a job at the Montgomery Ward in Cheshire selling fishing and camping gear. When her husband died of lung cancer five years ago, she was glad to have the extra income from the little rental over the garage.

Now, as I started up the stairs to the apartment, I heard her screen door bang. She carried a small plastic trash bag out to her can in the driveway.

"Oh, I didn't see you," she said, eyebrows raised with innocence. "Everything okay?"

I nodded. "Just another long night at work."

"Oh gosh, and I was hoping maybe you were out having fun with a guy."

"There was a guy. But it was work-related."

She walked over closer to me and leaned on the railing.

"You know, I'm going out with a fireman. Lots of nice single guys down there at the station. Maybe we could introduce you."

I shook my head, thinking about how limited my options were for a social life in this town.

"Maybe somebody from another town. Anybody connected to West Wicklow is sort of off limits for me."

She wrinkled her brow, then after a moment relaxed it. "Ah, I get it. You can't be too cozy." Her face brightened. "Well, we'll have to find somebody in Cheshire. I'll ask Lonnie to keep his eyes open."

That night, I lay awake until past two, mind restless, pieces of this new life flashing by like movie scenes in fast-forward.

I suddenly wished my father was just down the hall. For most of my life, it had been just him and me, but his presence was so immense that my world always felt full. He was "the" Colin Sullivan after all, a civil rights lawyer of some notoriety in Philadelphia, a ruddy-faced, giant block of a man, practicing in a cramped office he set up in the parlor of our rowhouse so he could keep a close eye on me after my mother died too young.

Now the silence of the bedroom pressed on my ears. I thought about a guy I dated in senior year. Marc Hampton. We went out on three dates. Slept together once. So glad to get that first awkward time out of the way. I was starting to feel that this might be the start of something. That I almost, possibly, was falling in love with him. Then over winter break, he went to Key West with a group of frat brothers and I got a postcard that said, "Let's remain friends but not dating partners." What a curious way to phrase it.

Even thinking of it now brought a dull gnawing in the chest, like heartburn. A painful reminder of my romantic ineptitude. I didn't know how to be a girl at all, let alone a woman. Some of my girlfriends talked about sitting with their mothers, sharing secrets, receiving wisdom about the ways of boys. I knew nothing about that whole world. Manicures. Eyeliner. How to make conversation with a guy. How to keep him.

I thought about a photograph of my mother that I still kept in my wallet, her hair red like mine but teased into a fiery bouffant. She was dressed to go out to a fancy event with Dad, wearing pearls around her neck and long white gloves. I was in first grade then, and I remember everything so clearly about that night. Her asking me to help her get ready. Sitting beside her at the dressing table in their bedroom on the delicate gold bench with the pink cushion. Me, so carefully handing her the perfume bottle she asked for, my little hands clutching the glass container like I would never let go. Dad snapping the picture. A year later she was gone.

I flipped over on my side and tried to plump my pillow. Must get to sleep. Lots to do tomorrow. Follow up on the mill story. Get ready for the council meeting protest that night. Start writing the profile on Eric.

I wasn't sure why I found it so easy to talk to him, when other guys left me tongue-tied. Maybe because I had the role of being a reporter to prop me up. I knew what to say, what to ask.

I thought again about Conrad Baines and Millicent, Darlene and Petey, and chided myself. I didn't come to West Wicklow to find a boyfriend. I came to find a story. Anything else was a distraction I couldn't afford.

Marty's comment about boxes of junk might point to some kind of insurance fraud scheme, or it might be nothing at all, a scene misinterpreted or misremembered by a highly unreliable witness. And even if that was a credible clue, how could it possibly relate to fires at thirteen different mills? Bob had told me they all had different owners. It all felt like a frustrating puzzle without a solution.

I thought back to the bits of advice Schramm had given in class. "By all means, 'follow the money,' as they famously did to uncover Watergate," he said once. "But even more importantly, follow the paper trail."

Schramm was an advocate of long hours spent pouring over government records. "It's tedious and not at all glamorous," he said, "but the payoff for all that tedium can be a monster story that no one else will find but you."

I resolved that tomorrow I would start pushing harder. Comb through every record I could find. Search for patterns, unexplained details, anything that could give me a place to start digging. No more worries about going slow and "building trust." I remembered Schramm's words. This was no time to be polite.

Chapter Six

At the police station the next morning, I grabbed the overnight reports from the basket and asked Teddy if I could also see the reports from all of the mill fires for the past year.

He arched an eyebrow.

"All of them?"

I nodded.

"Detectives Division has them," he said. "You'll have to ask Lieutenant Pelletier when you stop over there." He paused. "What do you want them for?"

I smiled. "Nothing in particular. Just want to know all the history, so I can do a good job."

He kept his eyes trained on me as I spoke. He had the look of a man who could punch you or bear-hug you at any moment. Tough to read.

"I'll let the Lieutenant know what you're looking for," he said, and returned his eyes to his paperwork.

Later, I stopped at Pelletier's desk. He had a quizzical smile.

"So, Miss Sullivan. Sounds like you're on a mission to turn our mill fires into the next Watergate. Am I right?"

I took a seat on the small metal chair next to his desk.

"Just trying to be thorough, Lieutenant."

He chuckled. "I'm just giving you a hard time. We'll get the reports pulled together for you. But it won't be today. We're a little backed up. Tomorrow afternoon, we'll have a box-full waiting for you."

"I appreciate it." I opened my notebook. "While I have you, anything new on the investigation of the Century fire?"

He withdrew a cigarette and lit it, taking a long drag.

"I wish I did," he said finally. "Our only working theory is still that vagrants are setting these, either accidentally or on purpose."

"Have you talked with any of them?"

"Who?"

"The vagrants."

He laughed out loud.

"Miss Sullivan, let me give you some advice. Why don't you leave the detective work to us?" About midway through that sentence, the temperature of his voice dropped about twenty degrees.

I flipped my notebook closed and stood up.

"Thanks again for making the reports available. I'll be back tomorrow."

"I'm sure you will," he called after me, "We'll be ready."

That evening, I arrived at Town Hall about a half-hour before the meeting to find a few dozen protestors already lining the sidewalk in front, a mix of all ages, some dressed in work uniforms, some carrying children, most of them waving handmade signs at passing cars. *Justice for Conrad. We Want Answers. Protect Us NOW!* The air was filled with raised voices, periodically erupting in chants of *Do Your Job, Do Your Job...*

I spotted Joel at the edge of the crowd, photographing a frail elderly woman holding a small sign that just said: *Help.* And there was Darlene in the middle of the crowd, hanging onto Petey with one hand, the other clutching a sign that said *Don't Let Our Lives Go Up in Smoke.* She saw me, too, and bobbed her head to say hello.

Just then I heard a murmur from the crowd and saw Eric standing at the top of the Town Hall steps.

"Everybody!" he shouted to the group. "They're going to be opening the doors to the Council Chamber now. Let's go in and fill up the front rows." The crowd started to stream toward the double doors. I slipped in among them.

I met up with Bob in the back of the chamber. Ned had assigned both of us to cover the protest as a tag-team. Bob would focus on the council members and the business of the meeting itself, while I'd gather quotes and color for a sidebar piece on the protestors.

"This is going to be interesting," he said to me in a low voice as I stood beside him. "The council is not exactly used to interacting with the public this way. Usually there's only a handful of regulars who attend these things."

I looked up at the raised dais in the front of the room where the seven council members sat on swivel chairs, a nameplate in front of each. In the center was Council President Tom Moreno, a short and stocky man with slick black hair, impeccably dressed in a dark blue suit with gold cuff links that gleamed when they caught the light.

I leaned over to whisper to Bob. "Moreno looks well-heeled."

He nodded. "Owns all the big GM dealerships here and in Wicklow."

"Must be the richest guy in town."

Bob shook his head. "Somebody's got him beat. Tell you later."

I wondered who that could be. To this point, I'd seen very little evidence of wealth in West Wicklow, not in the cars on the roads or the houses that lined the winding streets.

Moreno banged the gavel to start the meeting.

"Welcome, everyone," he said, his lips pursed into a thin crescent of a smile. "I see that we have many concerned citizens here tonight. Let me assure you, everybody who wants to speak will get their chance. But we do have to follow our published agenda, and there are several items before we get to the public comment period."

A murmur rose up from the protestors and Moreno quickly gaveled them back to silence. I glanced over at Eric. He sat impassive, arms folded.

The meeting began with a litany of mundane matters: acceptance of minutes from the last meeting, treasurer's report and congratulatory proclamations for town employees with more than twenty-five years of service. This included reading the names of all seventeen people, several of whom were in the audience and thus were asked to stand and be applauded. Following this was a lengthy reading of council by-law changes by the town solicitor, with subsequent commentary and questions from each of the council members.

I checked my watch. The meeting had been trudging on for just over an hour. One of the council's two female members, Nancy Boucher, swiveled fitfully in her chair, her forehead furrowed, as the next agenda item was called.

"Mr. President, may I be heard," she asked, leaning toward Moreno.

"Of course, Mrs. Boucher."

"Out of respect for the many citizens who have come out tonight to speak to us, I move that we suspend the agenda and begin the public comment period immediately."

A cheer erupted from the crowd. Moreno banged the gavel, scowling.

"I second!" said Councilman Daniel Silva, seated next to Boucher.

Suddenly a shout came from a young man in the front row.

Do Your Job!

The crowd repeated it, low at first and then intensifying, filling the chamber. Moreno glanced at the sergeant-at-arms who stood at the door, and I couldn't help but stare at the large sidearm prominently holstered on the cop's hip. The other council members sat stiffly with strickened expressions.

Eric stood up, motioning with his arms for quiet and the group hushed. Quickly Moreno called the motion, which passed unanimously.

Another cheer. One by one, the protestors walked to the microphone to speak for their allotted three minutes. Each had a story to tell of how the fires had impacted their lives.

Millicent's son from Florida was there, holding up a photo of her. The reverend from the Unitarian Universalist church, who knew Conrad from their soup kitchen ministry, described him as a "gentle soul who deserved better." The owner of a small auto repair business in one of the mills that burned earlier in the year talked about how he lost most of his customers in the aftermath and had to lay off his two mechanics.

Darlene came up next, Petey in her arms. She wore a waitress uniform—black slacks and a crisp white blouse—and her voice was strong and steady.

"A lot of you might have already read about my experience in the paper, so I won't spend time on that. I just want all of you to look at this little guy," she said, turning to smile at her boy. "He's my whole world. All I'm asking for is a safe place for him to grow up."

She paused, looking at each of the council members.

"I think you'd want the same for your children. Thank you."

After all had their say, Eric came to the microphone.

"We've come tonight not just to share stories of how these fires have affected the people of this town, but also," he said, slowing to emphasize his words, "to demand action."

"After thirteen fires over almost a year, it's not enough to say that the causes are undetermined or still under investigation," he continued, his voice taking on an edge. "We believe the council, as our elected body representing the people, needs to conduct its own inquiry, to finally figure out what is going on here, for the good of all the residents of West Wicklow."

The crowd cheered and once again Moreno gaveled them. Mrs. Boucher offered a motion that the council establish a task force to gather information and report back to the full body in thirty days.

The motion sparked derisive muttering sounds from the other members.

"What you're suggesting is to meddle in the work of our very fine police and fire departments!" said one. Moreno broke in.

"We have both chiefs here in the room tonight," he said. "Gentlemen, please come to the microphone and share your thoughts on this motion."

I glanced over to the corner of the room, just off the dais. There stood a cluster of town department heads, and from the center of the group emerged the two chiefs. I had seen each of them in passing as I made my daily rounds but had yet to officially meet either of them. Bob had told me they both kept a low profile, deferring to their next-level-down leaders, Lieutenant Pelletier and Battalion Chief Nunes, to speak to the media.

The two chiefs stood shoulder to shoulder at the microphone. Police Chief Rocco "Rocky" Recchia spoke first.

"I understand the frustration that everyone feels, but let me assure you that we are working day and night in coordination with the fire department to get to the bottom of these fires."

Recchia took a step back and Fire Chief Maurice Lambert leaned closer to the microphone.

"I concur completely with Chief Recchia. Everything that can be done is being done."

A councilman at the far end of the table turned toward Moreno.

"Mr. Council President, based on that, I believe a task force would be nothing but a grandstanding move to satisfy these protestors—and that's no way to run a town. I call the motion for a vote."

The motion failed, five to two, with Boucher and Silva as the only "ayes."

The vote brought a torrent of boos and a new chant from the protestors. They stood with their signs, pounding the wooden posts on the floor as they filed out into the darkness.

We'll Be Back! We'll Be Back!

The next day's paper gave the protest big play, with a bold headline running across all six columns at the top for Bob's lead story, Joel's photo of the woman carrying the *Help* sign, plus my color story on the protestors. Below the fold, Ned had positioned my sidebar on Eric under the headline: *Young Man on a Mission*. The

59

thumbnail photo of him was one I remember Joel snapping during the meeting: his eyes intense, jaw set.

At our staff meeting after deadline, we talked about where the story might head next.

"Those council members looked rattled," said Bob. He explained that Boucher and Silva represented the districts where all of the fires had taken place so far. "At the risk of a bad pun, I think they're feeling the heat."

Groaning ensued from the other reporters. I asked Bob why Moreno and the rest of the majority were so set against a task force.

"Moreno is a businessman," he said. "He wants everything to be smooth, no controversy that could hurt business. For months, he's complained to me that we're playing up these fire stories too much."

I told Ned about my plan to review police reports on all of the fires that afternoon.

"Good idea," he said. "The council doesn't want to take a close look, but we're sure as hell going to keep at it."

It was Maddie's turn to give her report. She drew in a deep breath first, a mannerism I'd noticed each time she had to speak in the meeting. It made me feel protective of her.

"Well, it's all about covering the Festa for me the next few days," she said. She pronounced it "Fesh-ta."

Everyone else nodded. I must have looked lost. Ned jumped in.

"Ah, that's right. Meg's new. Maddie, give a quick rundown on what Festa is all about."

Maddie proceeded to school me in the traditions of the Feast of the Holy Ghost or "Festa do Espirito Santa" in Portuguese. I learned it was the major annual event for the local Portuguese community, part solemn religious event, part carnival, commemorating the kindness of Saint Isabel, the queen of Portugal in the 1300s who distributed food to her country's poor. Maddie's family was active in the Portuguese Holy Ghost Society, which sponsored the festival each year on the grounds of its clubhouse on Main Street.

"Every Labor Day weekend, Festa pretty much takes over the town," Maddie said. Having the festival to talk about in the reporters' meeting seemed to make her blossom. "I'll be covering it from start to finish, so look for me if any of you come by."

"I'll stop by tonight," I volunteered. With a long weekend looming, I was glad to have somewhere to go.

"I'll point you toward the best food booths," she said. "My Aunt Ida's pepperoni bread is guaranteed to blow your mind."

When I arrived at the station that afternoon, Teddy led me down a long corridor to a windowless holding room. At a desk opposite the doorway sat a burly uniformed officer with a buzz-cut. He looked up from his paperwork, stone-faced.

Inside the room, two large cardboard file boxes sat on the table. Teddy left the door open as he left.

"When you're done, signal the officer outside and someone will escort you out." His voice was flat. While he'd never actually been friendly toward me, I noticed a definite chilliness that was new.

A fluorescent light above me that had been flickering suddenly came on full-force, making me jump in my chair. The uniformed officer looked up and stared, then turned back to his paperwork.

I began looking through the file folders on each fire, one by one. I had a game plan. First, to find information on the ownership of each mill. Second, to scour the reports for references to inventory damaged. And third, anything suspicious. Wasn't sure exactly what would be in that third category, but I figured I would know it when I saw it.

I remembered from reviewing the report on the Century fire that the ownership and contact information was written in a box in the upper right corner. I began laying out all the reports on the table. I could feel the officer's eyes on me as I stood with my pen and notebook in hand, circling the long table to copy the owners' names.

Bob was right—they were all different. All of them business names, no individuals. Wicklow Realty Partners. Frontenac Associates. A1 Distributors. Main Street Property Holdings. Thirteen different names. I copied down the contact phone numbers for each. They were all different, too, although all were local and many had the same first three digits.

I felt my heartbeat quicken. *Follow the paper trail.* Schramm would be proud. Today's digging would lead to more. I knew that in the state capital of Providence, in the Secretary of State's office, I'd be able to find incorporation papers for all thirteen companies that might tell me more. And at the right time, I would call all thirteen of those numbers and learn who was on the other end.

I spent the rest of the afternoon reading each report, taking careful notes. In every one, there were references to the owner reporting "substantial" or "extensive" losses of inventory in the fire. Eyewitness statements were few. A handful of small business tenants reported what time they had locked up the night of the fire and that they noticed nothing amiss.

Each of the file folders contained a follow-up report issued by the state Fire Marshal's office. I kept reading similar phrases in each. *Very little evidence found at the scene. No signs of an accelerant.* And on the line marked *Cause*, all said the same thing.

Undetermined origin.

I put the last of the folders back in its box and flipped my notebook closed. The officer looked up.

"Are you ready, miss?"

"Yes," I said. "I have everything I need."

When I came out of the station after five, the air was cool with a hint of autumn approaching. The Festa site was close enough to walk, and I was glad for the chance to clear my head.

Up ahead in the next block, throngs of people poured toward the festival site. I fell in with them, letting the smiles and chatter carry me along. I felt like an anonymous traveler, almost invisible, in a sea of people bound by family and affection and tradition.

The sound of young voices floated above us and the crowd hushed. In front of me, a choir of boys and girls in blue plaid Catholic school uniforms stood outside the Holy Ghost Society building, singing a hymn. The melody was familiar—the Ave Maria— with words that I was starting to recognize as the sound of Portuguese. In the open doorway, an altar boy in a white robe emerged carrying a tall gold cross, and behind him, six men in black suits shouldered a wooden platform holding the statute of Saint Isabel that Maddie had described, covered with roses of red, pink and white.

People in the crowd began to make the sign of the cross and I did the same. I thought back to the May Processions of my childhood, a blur of little girls in starched white dresses and lace veils, carrying a crown of roses for the statue of the Blessed Mother. For the first time since coming to this town, I felt a little less like an outsider.

The procession continued to the festival stage in the parking lot, where Saint Isabel would rest until Sunday morning, when another procession would take her to Mass at Our Lady of Perpetual Help Church across the street.

I stood in the middle of the festival grounds and turned slowly to take in every sight, sound and smell. It felt as though every single soul in West Wicklow had crowded into this one square block. Every one of them in high spirits.

Along one side were familiar small-town carnival rides. Teenagers shrieked as they crashed into one another in bumper cars. Kids and parents squealed on spinning rocket ships. A tame choo-choo train chugged along a tiny track, the cars stuffed with red-cheeked toddlers, their parents leaning on the picket fence surrounding it, waving and snapping pictures.

In the center was a midway with games of chance and tests of skill. The scene was one of constant motion and sound: hammers swung, bells rang, darts pierced balloons on a board with a "pop" like gunfire, wheels spun with a clickety-clickety-clack.

I breathed in deeply. An amalgam of smells both foreign and familiar emanated from a long row of food booths along the opposite side. Sweet cotton candy. Shaved steak and burgers sizzling alongside Italian and Portuguese sausages. The smell of the seashore carried on a light breeze, courtesy of mussels and clams simmering in giant kettles.

I spotted Maddie standing in front of a tent with a banner that proclaimed: *Pepperoni Bread!* in bold red letters.

"You made it!" she said, waving me toward her.

"This is amazing," I said.

"Have you eaten anything yet?"

I shook my head.

"Ha," she said, "then you haven't even gotten to the amazing part yet."

I waved hello to her mother, Rosie, inside the booth, and Maddie introduced me to the woman next to her who looked like Rosie's slightly older double.

"This is my Aunt Ida."

Ida smiled, but not broadly. She had a look of quiet decorum.

"I've heard all about you from Maddie," she said. "Your father is an attorney, I understand."

"Yes, in Philadelphia," I replied.

She cast her eyes down at the bread dough she was sternly pressing into shape.

"Well," she said, never looking up from her task, "we hope our Maddie doesn't ever move so far away from home."

"Now Ida…" Rosie said, nudging her gently with her hip. "This is a new world now. Not like when we were girls."

"How about trying some pepperoni bread," Maddie said quickly, pointing me toward a long tray bearing slices of bread with a filled center.

"I've heard that these are the best thing about Festa," I said, carefully using the proper fesh-ta pronunciation.

Ida's lips turned upward into a tentative smile.

I bit into a warm slice. Chunks of pepperoni and melted cheese filled my mouth with flavor.

"Unbelievable," I mumbled.

Ida's smile inched further upward.

"I would be happy to share my recipe with a friend of Maddie's," she said. With obvious pride, she began to describe how she prepared the bread. I pulled out my notebook and jotted down the instructions.

"Start with your bread dough." She leaned closer to me. "You can use the frozen dough. Don't tell anyone, but it really doesn't make much difference." Flatten it down and brush with half of a beaten egg. Lay down five or six slices of pepperoni, then another layer of American cheese. Fold the edges of the dough over and press down, like sealing an envelope. Brush the top with the other half of egg, sprinkle with sesame seeds, cover with a cloth and allow to rise. Bake at 350 degrees for twenty minutes.

"Try it sometime," she said. Her eyes had started to twinkle. "Just don't spread the recipe around. I've got a reputation to protect."

"You can trust Meg," Maddie interjected with a laugh. "A good reporter never reveals her sources."

I nodded solemnly. "That's right. Your secret is safe with me."

Maddie glanced at her watch.

"Oops, it's back to work for me. I've got to run now and interview the Festa queen before the ribbon cutting ceremony."

Ida beamed and reached over to pat my hand. "Did you know that our Maddie is a past Festa queen?"

"Aunt Ida," Maddie protested gently, "Meg doesn't want to hear about my glory days."

"I do, as a matter of fact," I said. "So, there's a queen?"

Rosie jumped in.

"Yes, the queen is chosen each year by the members of the society and she has a court made up of six girls who are the runners-

64

up. Everyone still says that Maddie was the most beautiful queen ever."

Maddie blushed.

"The queen and her court march in the parade on Sunday night and appear at other Festa events, like the ribbon cutting that will happen in just a little while up on stage," Rosie continued.

Maddie and I agreed to meet later by the stage and said our goodbyes to Ida and Rosie. I continued my wandering, passing a booth for Estrella's restaurant where I caught a glimpse of Darlene in the back dishing out steamed clams. I made a mental note to double back after the ceremony to say hello and have something to eat.

I entered a large tent with a maze of small booths inside featuring a mix of event sponsors and local nonprofit organizations. In the center sat a shiny red pick-up truck under a banner for Moreno's dealership that screamed in large letters: "Enter to Win!" About a dozen people crowded around a table, scribbling their names on slips of paper to drop into the entry bowl.

Up ahead, a middle-aged woman holding a baby stood in front of a booth with a banner for the Alliance for Social Justice. There behind the table was Eric. He stood with arms folded across his chest, listening to her talk. He pointed down to a clipboard on the table and handed her a pen to sign on the sheet of paper there. As she bent over to write, he looked up and spotted me. I waved and a smile started to appear in the corner of his lips but just then the woman asked him a question and he leaned over to talk to her.

At first, I thought I might linger, wait until he was free so we could talk, but then a few more people stepped up to the booth. For just an instant, an odd feeling shot through me. Was that disappointment? I was irritated with myself, getting all aflutter like a teenager. I imagined the words *I am your source* painted across his chest. It was probably best to move on.

Farther up the midway I spotted Francie spinning a wheel at a booth to benefit the West Wicklow Fire Department.

"I only know a few people in town but it seems like all of them are here," I said to her.

"That's West Wicklow for you," she said. "It's like we all live together in one room."

As dusk began to settle over the fairgrounds, I met up with Maddie at the foot of the stage. We watched as Council President

65

Moreno strode to the podium with other local dignitaries and cut a giant blue ribbon to officially open the festival. Once again, he was attired in a perfectly tailored suit, this one with a slight sheen when the stage lights played on it.

After the ceremony, Maddie headed off to conduct more interviews. Moreno caught my eye across the crowd and waved, signaling for me to come over. I was surprised. Didn't think he knew who I was.

"You're Meg Sullivan, aren't you?" he said, shaking my hand. "I saw you at the council meeting but we haven't had a chance to get introduced yet."

We exchanged some pleasantries. He said he'd been following my stories and was impressed. I felt slightly off balance as he continued to talk. Why would he approach me like this? And why would he compliment stories about the fires when Bob said that subject was a sore point for him?

The crowd pressed in on us, and people kept coming up to him to pat his arm or squeeze his shoulder. He motioned for me to follow him to a quieter spot a few steps away.

"I can tell from the way you go about your business that you're a very good reporter," he said in a low voice. "An ambitious reporter. I like ambition."

His mouth turned up in a way that looked partly like a smile, partly a grimace. He reached into his jacket pocket, withdrew his business card and handed it to me.

"Flip it over," he said.

On the back was written a phone number.

"You see, Meg, the problem is that West Wicklow is not a very big stage for someone like you. I have an old friend who owns a large paper in New Jersey, just a hop across the river from Manhattan. He's looking for a first-rate investigative reporter, so of course I immediately thought of you."

I stared down at the card, feeling my legs turn rubbery.

He put his hand on my shoulder. "The job is yours. Just make the call."

Chapter Seven

I walked through the Festa grounds only half-hearing, half-seeing. The multicolored lights and music and chatter flowed by in a world apart from mine, like watching sharks swim past your nose at the aquarium.

What the hell just happened?

I struggled to slow down the thoughts careening through my mind. And below all that chaos, something else, deep down.

Fear.

All of my old doubts came rushing back, the worries about not being tough enough to do this work. Maybe I'd stumbled onto something that was bigger than I could handle. And with more risk than I ever considered. I fingered the business card in my jacket pocket. All those months I'd hoped for a job offer to come through from a big-circulation newspaper in the New York market. Funny way to get your prayer answered.

I tried to analyze what Moreno did and all the things it could have meant. Had someone alerted him that I was poking into the old fire records? And since he clearly wanted me gone, was this just his way of quieting down bad publicity for his town? Or something more?

I realized I was walking back toward the paper. Ned would be there now, making preparations for the Saturday morning edition. That was a comforting thought. I could talk to Ned. I didn't have to figure this out all by myself.

"That son of a bitch!"

Ned snuffed out one of the two cigarettes he had working with a rough twist of his hand into a round tin ashtray. His bellowing voice shook the empty newsroom.

"In this little horseshit town. West Wicklow!" He shook his head. "Well, I shouldn't be surprised. People are people no matter how big or small the town. And people are corruptible. That's why people like us have jobs."

He paused and studied me.

"Are you OK?"

I wasn't sure how I was, actually. "Just a little rattled, I guess. It took me by surprise."

He sat back in his chair. "Now, I don't want you to take this the wrong way. But Meg, if you have any concerns—about your safety, I mean—nobody would blame you if you said, hey, I never signed up for this."

The minute he said those words I realized I wasn't looking for a way out.

"Nobody's going to run me out of this town," I said.

He smiled.

"Good. And remember, you're not alone. We'll figure out what these bastards are up to and nail them."

We talked for a while about strategy, what to do next, how to handle Moreno.

"If he corners you again, just kill him with kindness," Ned advised. "Say you've really grown to love the town and don't want to leave."

I nodded. "And meanwhile, I'll be working on the public records angle."

"Good." he said. "The records should point us in the right direction, but I think we're also going to need a source who's on the inside. There have to be people who know what's going on. Sometimes a person's conscience starts to nag at them. Talk to as many people connected with the town government as you can. Try to crack this nut open."

I slept restlessly that night and awoke early Saturday morning with remnants of a vivid dream clinging to my consciousness like a cobweb. I sat alone at a table in a cavernous library that could have been from Dickens' era, with dark wood paneling and ornate circular staircases leading to multiple levels. I started to climb the stairs to the mezzanine above, round and round, then suddenly found myself in a decrepit tower with crumbling stone steps that gave way under my feet.

Awake, I pulled gently at the dream fragments, wanting to remember not just the details, but what I felt as I climbed. I wasn't afraid. Inquisitive but careful, frustrated but not terrified. Maybe that could be my mantra for moving forward in this job, in this town.

The long weekend stretched out before me. Tonight I would stop by the Festa again and meet up with Maddie and some of the other reporters afterward. Francie invited me to her barbeque on Sunday. I'd make my weekly call to Dad Sunday night. That still left so many hours to fill.

I poked my head out the front door to check the weather. Perfect late-summer day. A light, warm breeze on the air. I decided to take a drive south to check out all of those little towns I'd seen on my map along the bay that led to the ocean.

Driving, windows down on both sides, seeing quick glimpses of blue water and sailboat masts pop out between thickets of trees and hedges, I felt the weight of my work start to slip away, carried off in the breeze. Frampton played a little louder than usual on my 8-track. The sun warmed my arm resting on the windowsill, my fingers tapping to the beat.

I crossed the town line into East Greenwich and spotted a sign that said "Launch Ramp" with an arrow to the left. I made a quick turn and followed the steep road down to the marina at the bottom.

Before me were perhaps a hundred sailboats packed side-by-side in their slips, their lines slapping against the metal masts in the breeze, creating a cacophony of chime-like sound. Beyond the marina was a sheltered cove with dozens more sailboats bobbing on moorings against the background of a densely forested peninsula. And where the cove emptied into the larger bay, dozens more sails dotted the water stretching out toward a hazy horizon.

I found a spot to park and headed toward the launching ramp, which was a jumble of activity. A truck backed a trailer carrying a small powerboat into the water while a multicolored catamaran worked its way toward the adjacent landing dock, its sails fluttering.

Seeing an uncrowded spot toward the end of the dock, I went over and sat down cross-legged to watch the scene. The wooden boards were warm beneath me and the salty breeze felt cool on my face. I adjusted my baseball cap to block the blinding sunlight bouncing off the water and the shiny fiberglass boat hulls.

Across the cove I saw a small sailboat working its way through the mooring field, scooting closely behind another boat, then changing course to clear the front of the next vessel. I lost sight of it for a time, then spotted it again further down the cove.

Now the boat bounded through an open stretch of water between the mooring field and the dock. The breeze picked up and the two small sails swelled, tipping it to one side, allowing me to get a better view. It was an open boat with a deep navy blue hull, perhaps halfway between the size of a dinghy and the smallest sailboats with cabins.

As it drew closer, for the first time I could see the sailor, a young man in a cap and sunglasses perched on the high side, steering with a long wooden tiller.

Wait. A flash of recognition, then disbelief. Surely Rhode Island couldn't be this small a state.

"Eric!" I shouted, waving my arms over my head.

He spotted me and looked dumbfounded for an instant, then broke into a wide grin. He glanced quickly behind him, then pulled on the tiller sharply to turn the boat toward the dock, sails fluttering in the wind as he guided it gently alongside.

"Seriously, will you reporters stop at nothing to get your story?"

I laughed. "Always on the job, hounding my sources."

He held the boat steady on the dock with his hand. Traces of a light sunburn colored his cheeks. The shaggy hair that hung below his cap flicked wildly in all directions in the breeze.

"Spectacular day for sailing," he said.

"I've been enjoying just watching everything. Never seen so many boats."

"You know, sometimes you have to stop being an observer, Meg."

He had that strange expression again, like he had at the diner that night, right before insisting we play the jukebox.

"Have you ever sailed?"

"Never."

"Would you like to?"

"Someday."

"How about right now?"

I was flustered. "I'm not sure I'm dressed for it."

He looked at my feet. "Not proper boat shoes, but sneakers will do. Hop in."

"Will it fit the two of us?"

"Yes, but I'll have to put you to work. C'mon."

I moved over to sit on the edge of the dock, my legs dangling into the boat, and he took my hand and guided me down to sit on the bench.

In an instant, he pushed off from the dock and pointed us toward the opening to the bay, sails puffing out to catch the wind. The sensation took me by surprise—a feeling of relinquishing control to

70

something outside me, a force gently pulling me through time and space, in perfect harmony with the natural world.

I glanced back at Eric and caught him studying me.

"It's amazing, isn't it?" he said. "I love watching first-timers."

I nodded. The waves slapped against the hull with a gentle, rhythmic beat. The deep blue of the water and smell of salt in the air were intoxicating. My muscles relaxed and I let myself slump casually against the rail.

"Don't get too comfortable," he said. "We're going to tack in a minute."

I'd heard the term but had no idea what it meant. He gave me a quick course in the principles of sailing. We can't sail directly into the wind, so we tack or "come about," back and forth in long sweeps, gradually making headway toward our destination. The lines (what I would call ropes) attached to the smaller sail in the front, called the jib, have to be released from the thimble-shaped "winch" on one side and cranked in on the opposite side when we tack.

"All of that will be your job," he said.

I steeled myself. Didn't want to look like an idiot, or worse, spill us into the bay.

"Ready about!" he shouted and gestured with his hand for me to unspool the line on the low side. As I did, the untethered sail started to flutter in the breeze and the line snapped around the cockpit like a crazed snake.

"Helm's a-lee," Eric yelled over the commotion, pushing the tiller in a controlled arc toward the opposite side. The jib flip-flopped its way across and I grabbed the line on my side, wrapping it quickly around the winch, losing my balance as the sail quickly filled with air and the boat leaned over on that side. I tottered backward and landed with a thud on the seat next to Eric on what was now the high side.

"Hard landing, but otherwise well done!" he said.

I could feel my cheeks flushing. Growing up in a big city, I'd never been exposed to adventurous outdoor sports, but I liked this feeling of mastering the wind, making it take us where we wanted to go.

We kept going for a time on a long tack, past the tip of the wooded peninsula that sheltered the cove where we'd started out. All before me was blue water to the horizon.

"Are we headed to Portugal?" I asked.

"Nah, we'd need a little bigger boat for that." Behind the reflector sunglasses, his expression was difficult to read. Only the slight curve upward in the corner of his mouth gave him away. I was beginning to appreciate his sense of humor. Like mine, a little off center.

"I thought we'd land on the beach over there," he said, pointing to a ribbon of sand stretching along the shore of the peninsula that lay open to the bay.

As we drew closer, Eric steered toward the wind, fluttering the sails to slow our speed. I looked over the side and suddenly saw bottom, sandy and speckled with shells.

"Prepare to raise the centerboard, matey," he said, gesturing toward a wooden handle in the center of the boat. I pulled upward and drew out a long wooden board, dripping with sea water, just as the boat skidded up onto the sand.

I climbed out clumsily, while Eric hopped onto the sand in one effortless motion and dragged the boat up higher on the beach, out of reach of the lapping waves.

"First rule of small boat seamanship," he said solemnly. "You never want to head off for a walk on the beach and look back to see your dinghy sailing off by itself to..."

"To Portugal?"

He laughed. "Exactly."

We began walking along the water's edge. The beach was empty except for a large seagull standing sentry ahead of us. As we approached, the bird suddenly bent its head back and let out a loud, cackling cry.

"I think he wants this beautiful place all to himself," I said, looking around at the panorama of sky and water in varying shades of blue, one melting into the next.

"I just discovered it a couple of weeks ago," Eric said. "Over there where you see all the trees is a state park. Then there's a handful of houses here on the point, but so far I've never seen a single soul on this stretch of beach. I come here sometimes just to sit and get my head straight."

I saw a large chunk of driftwood ahead.

"There's my bench!" he cried.

It was just long enough for the two of us to perch side by side. How natural it felt to sit there, with the salt breeze blowing back our hair, watching the boats make their way against the wind. West Wicklow had become a distant solar system.

We sat there for a time. No words exchanged, none needed. Once, when I looked out toward open water, his head was turned in that same direction and I found myself studying his profile: his features perfectly proportioned like sculpture, his gaze steady and thoughtful. To this point in my life, every guy my age had been a boy. But here was a man. A fine man, I thought. There was something admirable about a person who could just sit and take in a scene like this, to appreciate its beauty, not needing to fill up the silent space with words.

Finally, he turned to me.

"How is the town treating you, Meg?" His voice had a weariness to it, like an invitation to share a burden weighing on us both.

I didn't answer immediately, uncertain about how much I could say.

He continued. "For me, I've found it to be a difficult place. I thought it would be a great feeling, being on my own, doing work that I loved. But it's more like I'm all alone, slogging uphill carrying a hundred-pound weight."

It was like hearing my own experience played back to me.

"I know the feeling," I said. "The deeper I get into my reporting about the fires, the more I feel like maybe I'm not the best person to uncover what's happening. It feels bigger than me."

"Don't say that!" The forcefulness of his reply took me by surprise. "You're tough, you're so smart, you're..." His sunburned face flushed redder. "You're amazing, Meg."

Our faces were so close together I could see the tiny creases at the corners of his eyes, smell the soap on his skin. He reached over and held the upper part of my arm, pulled me toward him and kissed me. In that moment, I forgot I was a reporter, forgot he was a source, forgot I was in Rhode Island. I was in a small capsule for two adrift on a blue sea, where there was every reason in the world to lean into the deepest kiss I'd ever had.

When it ended, I felt myself reverting to awkward Meg. "This is probably not such a good idea," I said, pulling back slowly.

He looked stricken. "I'm sorry...I thought..."

"No, no...not that it was a bad idea. It was a really wonderful idea," I stammered, and his face softened.

"It's just that," I continued, "I'm working this story, and you're an important player in the story."

He hung his head and nodded. "I understand. The way the town fathers operate, they could use it against us, make things ugly."

"Yeah, I've already gotten a taste of the ugly part," I said, and then instantly wished I hadn't. I knew I shouldn't say anything about Moreno's attempt to get rid of me.

"What, did somebody from the town give you a hard time?" he asked. He looked worried for me, and I liked it.

"I can't really talk about the details, since I don't have enough to accuse anybody of anything, but let's just say someone tried to encourage me to leave town."

He let out a low whistle. "God."

Then he turned and put his hands on my shoulders, gazing straight into my eyes.

"Meg, don't push me away completely. Let's work together where we can. Let's try to get to the bottom of this thing, where it leads. And when it's over, when there's nothing stopping us, then…"

I nodded. The irony was staggering. Finally, to experience this feeling that everyone talks about, dreams about. And I'm in the wrong place at the wrong time with an incredibly right guy.

"I should get you back to the mainland," he said. We stood up and walked slowly back along the water's edge. He took my hand and we hung on until we reached the boat.

"The wind will be behind us now all the way back," he said, pushing the boom that carried the large mainsail out ahead of us until it filled with air and we hopped in.

"This is one of the fastest points of sail," he said, continuing my lesson. "Coming here, that was called beating, where you're tacking close to the wind. When the wind's coming from the side, that's called a reach."

I felt the breeze pushing the boat faster, making the water gurgle at the bow as we gained speed.

"And what's this called, with the wind at our back?" I asked.

He smiled wryly.

"Running," he said. "We're running."

Chapter Eight

The rest of September passed without another fire. I wondered if my poking around had prompted the guilty parties to lay low. The days turned crisp under cloudless blue skies and the nights grew cold enough for me to fire up the electric baseboard heaters in my apartment.

I kept digging. Eric helped me find and interview dozens more men who had been sleeping in the mills. Four of them provided information similar to what Marty had told me: that they saw boxes moved in the night before the fires. Two of them had looked inside and saw the same thing: a mishmash of used, worthless-looking clothes and household goods.

I spent hours at the Secretary of State's office in Providence looking through their registry of businesses incorporated in Rhode Island, filling up nine notebooks with the names of the officers of the mill-owning companies and their attorneys.

Ned noticed me at my desk one quiet afternoon flipping through the growing stacks of notebooks as I tried to start analyzing all the data I'd found.

"You're going to need a big board where you can map out everything and begin to see the whole picture," he called to me across the empty newsroom.

I stood up and went over to his desk.

"Is that how you did it at the *Courier-Journal*?" I asked. I leaned against the file cabinet, trying to look casual. I wanted to learn from him, but I knew he rarely talked about his experiences as a reporter—or his personal life at all, for that matter. None of the reporters knew much more about him than the bit of gossip Bob had told me. Only that he lived alone in an apartment around the corner from the paper.

His face darkened for an instant, like a passing cloud. He lit a cigarette and leaned back in his chair.

"Haven't thought about those days much. Seems like a lifetime ago." He pushed the smoke out through pursed lips like he was expelling a demon. "There were two of us who worked on investigative stories. We had a room that became our command center, where we kept all of our files. Our building had originally been an elementary school, and an old chalkboard ran the whole length of one wall. We used it to diagram the key players, timelines. It helped us put it all together."

"Was that how you worked on the series about the slumlords?"

"Ah, so you've heard about my illustrious resume." He took a long puff, his expression a jumble of pride and shame.

"The only bad thing about winning a Pulitzer is that you've won a goddamned Pulitzer. And then it's, okay, what's your Act Two? I guess the pressure got to me."

His eyes narrowed, as if he just realized he was talking out loud to another person.

"Now I see how you get so much information out of people," he said, shaking his head and taking another puff.

"But everything's okay for you now?"

He nodded. "Yep. Thanks to some meetings I go to. And a guy who's sort of my…" He was searching for a word to describe it, but I already knew.

"Your sponsor."

He looked surprised. "So you know about this stuff."

"An uncle of mine. Twelve years sober last month. It saved his life."

He stood up and stubbed out his cigarette. It felt like he was gently closing a door he hadn't meant to open.

"I have to admit, it feels good to let somebody know about it," he said, looking down at me over the tops of his wire-rims. "But this is about you and your story. We need to get ourselves organized like a real investigative operation. Ruskin told me there's a room up on the third floor that we could use if we ever needed it. Let me check into it."

A couple of days later, Ned dropped a key on my desk.

"Go up and take a look. See if it's a place where you can work."

The room smelled musty, but had a large window that let light stream in. In one corner sat a tall wooden filing cabinet and, in the center, a wooden table and chair. On all four walls, someone had carefully taped giant sheets of cream-colored commercial wrapping paper. Another roll of the paper stood in the corner with a plastic tape dispenser sitting on top. A pile of felt markers in different colors lay on the floor.

I took it as a sign that Ned thought this story was worth the effort. I wished I understood more about how things had gone so wrong for him in Louisville.

Winning a Pulitzer was something I started dreaming about back at Oakmont. The ultimate recognition that you had produced work that was important, work that helped uncover an injustice or solved a problem. Ned's story flashed like a caution light in front of me. Just keep focusing on the work. Push everything else away. Ambition. The desire for applause. Fear of being a flash in the pan. The only thing that matters is the story.

I set a routine for myself. Mornings, the normal flow of stories, writing on deadline. In the afternoons and evenings, I covered any other breaking news and regular public meetings on my beat. I spent most of the waking hours that remained in the room upstairs.

The other reporters had taken to calling it "the war room." Each of them would stop by now and then to see how my multicolored markings on the wall were progressing, sometimes offering a word of advice or raising a question that hadn't yet crossed my mind.

I'd transferred all of the key details on the thirteen fires onto the long wall on one side of the room. I drew thirteen large circles around the perimeter. Each circle contained all of the key information on that fire. I left the center of the wall blank, hoping to eventually draw lines between related details that would begin to reveal a pattern.

One afternoon, Bob stopped by just as I was beginning to look for connections among the names of corporate officers and attorneys that had been listed in the state registry for each of the mill-owning companies.

"Interesting," he said as he moved from circle to circle, examining the names. "So the cast of characters is different for each mill…"

"…and yet," I continued, "certain characters pop up again and again in different roles. Manuel Perreira, Esq. was the attorney for three of the companies." I pointed with my finger each place his name appeared. "But our friend Manny is also listed as secretary for three other companies and treasurer for two more."

Bob moved closer to the wall. "And Robert Chambord's name appears here, here and again down here," he said, tapping the name as he followed the trail. "Bob and Manny are partners in the biggest and most prestigious law firm in town: Perreira Law Associates. They tend to be the ones who represent the movers and shakers in town."

My mind was racing ahead. "That reminds me of something I've been meaning to ask you. Remember at the town council hearing on the fires? I'd asked if Moreno was the richest guy in town and you said, no, somebody else has him beat. Who's that?"

Bob had a look in his eyes like his mind was jumping ahead too.

"That would be Roland Ducharme. He's a businessman with his hands in lots of things in town. Ever driven past the country club up on the hill?"

"Sure. My apartment is just around the bend from there."

"That's his house, or I guess I should say mansion, at the crest of the hill, opposite the golf course entrance."

I remembered seeing a driveway with two towering stone pillars connected by an iron gate. I could never quite see the house itself, just glimpses of brick and stone amid thick stands of pine trees.

Bob explained that Ducharme's father owned a small shoe factory on the outskirts of town. When he died, Roland parlayed that money into buying and selling businesses.

"Keeps a low profile," Bob said. "He has an office in the Medeiros Building on lower Main. I've seen him just a handful of times out walking. People are always pointing fingers like, 'hey, that's him.'

"His money is behind a lot in the town, like Split Rock Estates, that big development across the line in Cheshire. In fact..." Bob paused as though reaching back into his memory, "there was a lawsuit a few years back. One of the homeowners sued over a drainage issue. Perreira was Ducharme's attorney. I remember interviewing him."

We looked at each other.

"This is all interesting," I said, "but the trouble is, Ducharme's name is nowhere on my wall."

"And," Bob added, "we have to remember this is a small town. There are only so many attorneys and other professional people of means. It makes sense that you're going to see the same names over and over."

I took a deep breath. "I just have to keep at it. Next, I've got to find out whatever I can about all of these people."

Bob looked down at his feet. "You know, I've never worked on a real investigative story. How about if I volunteer to help you run some of this information down? At least fill in some of the town history and relationships that I know?"

I suddenly felt a few pounds drop from my shoulders.

"That would be a huge help. Just what you've given me today has been so valuable."

He paused as he headed toward the door. "I feel a little bad that I covered all of these fires before you came and never really dug in the way you have. I think you're really onto something."

I smiled. "I just had the advantage of coming in with fresh eyes. But you have the advantage of knowing this town inside and out. Together, we might just be able to solve this."

The hours I spent alone in the war room during that time helped to calm and focus me. So much of my workday was spent interacting with other people, hustling back and forth to public meetings, doing phone interviews. In the room, all was quiet. I could study the information I had gathered and let my mind process what it all might mean. A trace of mustiness lingered in the room, and I had taken to opening one of the windows a crack to let some fresh air in while I worked. The low hum of passing cars, birdsong and street chatter filtered through the opening. I was still part of the world, yet separate. I marked the passage of time by the slant of the afternoon sun as it lit up patches of my handwritten notes across the wall.

Working in this kind of solitary state was not unfamiliar to me. Growing up, I treasured time alone in my bedroom to do schoolwork, listen to music or just daydream. Sometimes, when I would visit the homes of my school friends who had brothers and sisters—younger ones shouting and racing about, older ones scolding or protecting—I wondered how different my life might have been with siblings. With a mother who stayed healthy and strong, filling up our rowhouse with kids. I imagined bunk beds and a little sister. Instead, I had a quiet house and a room of my own. I suppose that became my normal.

My pattern of working in the war room had sparked some chatter among the *Times* employees.

"You know, you're the talk of the press room," Maddie told me once, passing along what she had heard from Rosie. "The guys downstairs don't know what to make of you. They think you've got some kind of bubbling cauldron that you're stirring up there."

One afternoon, I heard slow footsteps on the stairs, then a knock.

"Meg," I heard a voice say. "It's Sandy Frazier. May I come in?"

"Of course!" I said, rising to meet him as he opened the door and stepped inside.

I had exchanged maybe two dozen words with Sandy since joining the staff. *Nice weather, isn't it?*—that sort of pleasantry. As the sports editor he operated in his own orbit, covering local games in the evenings and weekends, writing stories in the far corner of the newsroom that was his domain. Bob described him as a "legend" who knew generations of West Wicklow families. He appeared to be in his early sixties, and yet he had the slight build and quick, darting movements of a ball-handling point guard on a high school basketball team.

"I was curious to see what all this 'war room' stuff is about," he said. "Mind if I take a look?"

"Be my guest," I said. I trailed a step or two behind him as he surveyed my wall of notes. As was his habit, he carried a pipe in his right hand and the slightly sweet aroma quickly filled the room.

As he went along, he murmured softly.

"Ah huh." Then a few steps.

"Huh." Side steps.

"Hmm."

Then a deep breath.

"This is all information from the various public records," I stammered, trying to fill in the great, discomfiting void of spoken words in the room. "Secretary of State's office, police reports. Some from phone interviews that Bob and I did…" I let my voice trail off.

He stood there for a time, scratching his chin.

"Lots of important people up on that wall," he said when he finally spoke. "A lot of good people." He paused. "A lot of good families." He emphasized that last word as if underlining it in red.

He looked around the room, then studied me closely. His expression wasn't angry or challenging. More like the focused gaze of someone trying to figure out a puzzle.

"Don't get me wrong," he said. "If somebody committed a crime, let's nail them. But I hate to see any innocent people get swept up along the way."

I struggled for words to reassure him that I would be careful, but came up empty.

He began to turn toward the door, then stopped and looked back at me.

"Clive says you're one of the best reporters he's ever seen come through here. That you really know your stuff."

"All I can do is keep following the facts," I said.

He nodded—quick, short head-nods, as if to say, *yeah, I got it.*

"And, I guess, all we can do is trust you."

In those early days of September, the face I most looked forward to seeing appear in the doorway of the war room was Maddie's. She had a habit of bringing coffee back with her when she returned to the newsroom after covering a story in the afternoon. One day, she appeared in the upstairs room with an extra one for me.

"You deserve a break, Meg," she said. "All these scribbles are enough to make you go blind."

So began the first of many coffee-fueled conversations. Maddie was like a sponge when it came to learning about the craft of journalism. She strolled around the room, asking where I found the various pieces of information and how I knew where to look for them in the first place.

"Are you telling me that all of this came from public records? Amazing," she said, shaking her head. She frowned. "I'm beginning to think my Mass Media course is lacking something. Just counting the months until I can transfer to a real journalism program at URI."

I was impressed with Maddie's stories in the paper. Despite being limited to light, heartwarming features—*At 101, Town's Oldest Resident Still Remembers Washboards, Buggies and the Turn of the Century*—she wrote in a lively voice, rich with detail and insightful quotes, which I took as evidence that she was quite skilled at extracting information from people. I believed she could be a very good reporter, assuming she could overcome her family's objections. But she didn't have one huge advantage I had—being sent to a college with a solid journalism program. I resolved in that moment to do everything I could to support her. Women should stick together. We had enough obstacles in our way.

"I've kept some of my books from college," I said. "You're welcome to borrow them anytime if you want."

"I will definitely take you up on that!" she said. Maddie had an exuberant way of speaking that was infectious. Spending time with her gave me a jolt of energy and optimism. And it felt good to chit-chat with another girl again. Hadn't kept in touch with my old college pals like I thought I would.

"Do you know what we should do?" Maddie asked, looking up from the coffee cup she had cradled in her hands, her eyes squinting as if formulating a plan.

"What?"

"Well, my days off at the *Times* are Tuesday and Wednesday, so I've clustered my classes on those days, but my Wednesday afternoons are wide open. And you always have one of your school board or zoning meetings on Wednesday nights, right?"

"Right, so I can take off on Wednesday afternoons, but usually I end up coming in here…"

"No! We should make Wednesday afternoons our day to go out and have some fun." She began to sing a variation on the old feminist anthem. "*We are women, hear us roar…*"

I had to laugh. Maybe it was not too late to have a kid sister after all.

Our Wednesday junkets over those next few months were a mental escape from all of the troubling things swirling in my life. One Wednesday in September while the weather was still warm, we drove south to Scarborough Beach, a vast expanse of white sand and lacy scallops of surf that is packed blanket-to-blanket on a summer weekend but was open and tranquil on this weekday. We sat with our low-slung folding chairs near the water's edge, talking for hours. She was dating a guy from school but said he probably wasn't "the one."

"I don't have that swept away feeling," she said. "What about you?"

I wished I could confide in her about Eric but it was all so uncertain and complicated and definitely not a good idea. "I guess I'm still waiting for 'the one' too," I said, and left it at that.

"Meanwhile, we have these great careers," she said. She shifted on her chair to face me. "I've been thinking about TV lately. Sometimes when I'm out covering events I'll run into reporters from the Providence stations. The women always look so perfectly put together. Cool and confident. Do you think I might have a chance to get a job like that someday?"

Television! My heart fell. I hoped she would aspire toward serious newspaper reporting. Reporters on TV had only a few minutes to tell a story. For me, it seemed so limiting. Then I quickly chided myself. This was about Maddie, not me. I needed to encourage her, not throw cold water on her budding dream. "Of course you could," I said firmly. "You're getting great experience now at the *Times*. "I think you're a really good writer, and let's face it, you would look and sound terrific on TV."

She scrunched up her face. "That's sweet of you, but I also get really nervous speaking in front of people. God, when I was Festa Queen and had to say a few words on stage I almost passed out from fright!"

"That's something you can work on. It gets easier the more you do it. I used to be too shy to open my mouth, but I just kept pushing myself to do things that scared me."

She looked surprised. "You were shy? *You?* Wow, maybe there is hope for me after all."

Chapter Nine

When I moved to Rhode Island in August, Dad was adamant he wouldn't come up to visit until the leaves changed color.

"You need a little space and time to spread your wings without me hovering over you," he said during one of our first weekly calls.

I'd thought about calling him the night Moreno made his offer. I remembered when I was little and afraid of some real or imagined monster, he would fold me in his big arms, safely pressed against the solid expanse of his chest, feeling the steady meter of his beating heart. But now, things were different. I needed to rely on myself to chase the monsters.

By early October, the leaves on the maple tree in Francie's front yard had turned a tawny mix of yellows and burnt orange. "They say the middle of this month is peak color here," I told him on our next call. "It's time."

He took the early Amtrak train the next Saturday and I met him at the station in Providence. It had been just two months since I'd seen him but as he emerged from the platform I realized what a poor substitute my memories of him had been these past weeks.

"There's my girl," he said, wrapping me in an embrace that quieted my every anxious thought.

We took a tour of the landmarks in my new life, stopping first at my apartment, where he looked like a giant in a dollhouse, then a spin through the deserted newspaper office.

He lingered for a while at my desk, as if trying to imagine my daily routine.

"Whenever I read the local news in the Philly papers now, I think about you," he said. "If there's a tough crime story or some controversy at a city council meeting, I wonder what it's like for you, doing this job." He paused. "You know, you haven't told me much about what you've been covering."

He was right. I didn't want to worry him. And, in truth, I still didn't know exactly what I was covering.

"Let's go take a ride and look at the leaves," I said, tugging at his sleeve. "We can talk about everything that's been happening. I could use your advice."

About a half-hour from West Wicklow lay the woodsy town of Scituate, home to a large natural reservoir that fed pure water to most of the state. I'd gone along with Joel and Sara one Sunday in September for a ride to scavenge for antique shop treasures. At that point, the leaves were just starting to turn.

Now, as I drove with Dad along the same winding route, the trees were infused with every shade of red, orange and yellow, and the late afternoon sun lit up the colors like a theater spotlight as we rounded each curve from shadows into the light. In my side vision, I could see him craning his neck and twisting in his seat to stare at each new explosion of color.

"If for no other reason, I will always be glad you moved to New England so I could see this amazing sight," he said.

"Well, that's one good thing about the move." As the words left my mouth I immediately wished I could pull them back in. I hadn't meant to sound quite so glum.

He looked over at me. "What's wrong, kiddo? Aren't you happy here?"

Happy wasn't a word that I'd thought a lot about. But when he asked it that way, straight out, I realized for the first time that, no, I wasn't happy. Not even close. But maybe starting out in a job like this, in circumstances like these, happy was not on the menu.

I began to tell him everything. About the fires, the challenges to getting information. About Darlene and Petey and all the others in harm's way. When I talked about Eric and interviewing the men in the mills, I could sense him tensing, shifting in his seat.

"You need to be careful, you know," he said quietly, turning his head to view the leaves.

"Don't worry." I was going to tell him next what had happened with Moreno but decided to wait.

After a time, he asked about Eric. "Sounds like he's been a great help to you."

I nodded. "He reminds me a lot of you, actually. Passionate about trying to help people who aren't getting a fair shake."

We had stopped at the only traffic light in Scituate, waiting as a young couple holding hands practically danced across the street, their teenage affection spilling out with every step.

"Any romantic possibilities? With Eric, I mean."

I glanced over and his face had that same awkward expression I'd seen so many times growing up. Dad trying to be a confidante. Trying to be a mom.

"For now, he's my source, so it can't go anywhere. But someday, maybe."

He reached over to pat my shoulder.

"The work is important. But so is having a life." He paused and smiled. "Saving the world can be a lonely job, you know."

Something about his tone of voice caught me and I suddenly saw scenes from my childhood flash by like photos taken from a different vantage point. After my mother died, Dad was always a solitary figure in those scenes. Devoted to me and to his work. Now I was starting to understand what it meant to be navigating through life alone.

We stopped at a rustic coffee shop that had a small wooden deck overlooking the wide reservoir. I ordered two hot ciders and we sat down at a picnic table, warming our hands around the paper cups. The afternoon sun had weakened and a profound chill enveloped us, our breath mingling with the steam rising from our cups. The water, bright blue and foreboding, looked as though it could turn a person to ice in a moment.

I asked Dad what was new back home.

"Actually, I do have some surprising news. Unless you've already heard it from your Oakmont friends. Sister Eveline is leaving the order."

The words shook me like a clap of thunder from a cloudless sky. Sister Eveline Schott was president of Oakmont and a firebrand for social justice causes, famously arrested in an anti-war protest on the steps of the Philadelphia Museum of Art in the early seventies. Dad had defended her successfully at trial and they'd remained friends ever since. He would take her out to Sunday dinner once a month to some off-beat place he wanted to try. On one particular Sunday soon after my graduation, all three of us met at an Indian restaurant and Sister entertained us with stories about her missionary work in Calcutta years before.

Sister had a presence that was almost regal. Tall and fair, she used to stride through the halls of Oakmont like a strict but benevolent queen, pausing to offer her warm smile or the dreaded furrowed brow of disapproval. On that evening in the candlelit restaurant, she looked effortless and elegant, with her pixie-cut hair and a short strand of pearls around her neck.

I remembered that night as an especially low point for me. She asked about my job search and I was beginning to feel pitiful for having such a complete absence of prospects.

"Don't ever give up your calling in life, Meg," she said firmly, leaning toward me. "You must persist. Don't let anything stop you." Those words helped me keep going. Now they made me wonder what could have possibly happened to change her own path.

"Why did she leave?" I pressed Dad for answers. "Do you have any idea?"

He shook his head. "We talked about it several times without really talking about it. She said she had come 'unmoored' from her calling. That's the expression she used. And that she was in a no-man's land between two worlds."

We moved on to other subjects, but my thoughts kept returning to the news about Sister. Of all the nuns I'd encountered in the course of my school years, she was the last one I could imagine leaving the order. When my story about John Harrington was published in the college paper, she sent me a handwritten note on a card with a simple cross embossed on the front. Inside she wrote:

Jesus said, "whatsoever you do for the least of my brethren, that you do unto me." Your story reminded me that He is among us every day, if only we'll open our eyes and our hearts. God bless you.

I'd felt unsettled when I read it, and even more so now thinking back. Despite sixteen years of Catholic schooling from first grade to college, I was far from devout. I rarely attended Mass during college and not at all since coming to Rhode Island. But I still thought of the faith as a part of me, and a part of my reporting work, an inner framework that helped guide what was right and wrong, just and unjust. If Sister could come "unmoored" from her calling, what did that mean for mine?

Before Dad left on Sunday, I took him out to dinner at Estrella's, the Portuguese restaurant where Darlene worked. I'd stopped there a few times since interviewing her and she always insisted on seating me at one of her tables.

She spotted us standing in line at the hostess station and swooped in.

"I have your table right over here," she said, guiding us into our seats in front of the window. When I introduced her to Dad, her eyes went wide and she leaned toward him.

"You must be real proud of your daughter," she said. "She's a good reporter but also a really good person, so I imagine you had something to do with that."

I cringed but Dad just beamed and then asked what she'd recommend on the menu.

"Well, for a special appetizer, you can't beat the Bombeiro. It's Portuguese sausage called chourico (which she pronounced *sha-REECE*, as all the locals did). We serve it in a little ceramic grill shaped like a pig and then set it on fire at your table. It's the best thing you will ever eat."

"I have to agree," I added. "I had it the first time I was here and order it every time now. It's like an addiction."

"Bombeiro it is, then," he said with a flourish. We ordered my other favorite: an unlikely sounding but divine combination of pork, littleneck clams and potatoes. And a bottle of Portuguese rosé. I felt like I was crossing some bridge to adulthood, ordering wine with my father.

When Darlene returned with the appetizer, she pulled a book of matches from her pocket. She shot me a look, as if to say, *yeah, I get the irony*. She lit the match and touched it to the pool of Sterno underneath the fat roll of burgundy-colored sausage, and in an instant the flames shot upward, sparking a collective "Ooo!" from the diners near us.

Just then I looked across the dining room and spotted Lieutenant Pelletier sitting at a table alone, staring right at me. Another one of those small world, small town sightings that happened every day in West Wicklow. A slight smile crossed his lips and he raised his wine glass, tilting it in my direction.

"Is that a friend?" Dad asked, carving off a piece of the charred chourico.

"Haven't figured that out yet. But if I had to bet, I'd say probably not."

That evening I dropped Dad off at the train station and headed back to West Wicklow as night fell. Driving up the hill toward my apartment, I heard the faint sound of sirens wailing. I rolled down my window, trying to determine the direction of the sound as the icy air blasted me.

At the top of the hill, I pulled into the driveway and saw Francie at the front door.

"Lonnie just left," she yelled. "It's Valley Mill this time. Sounds like a big one."

The Valley fire was aggressive, jumping across a narrow road and igniting the adjacent three-decker so quickly that residents on the upper floors were trapped inside. Six people were transported to the hospital, some with severe burns, others with injuries from leaping onto a porch roof to escape. A firefighter was treated for smoke inhalation after climbing inside a third-story apartment to rescue a two-year-old girl.

By the time I reached the scene, most of the ambulances had left and I focused on gathering the facts from Battalion Chief Nunes and some residents standing across the street.

"It happened so fast," said a tall man with a blanket over his head that he clutched tightly around his body. "We only made it out because we were on the first floor," he said, pointing at his wife sitting on the lawn, holding one young son in each arm as they cried. "Thank God we're safe, but what about the others? What the hell is happening in this town?"

At the edge of the crowd I saw a pair of women in Red Cross caps assisting the victims. Beside them was Joel, his face ash-streaked and weary, writing down the names of a couple he'd just photographed. And there next to him was Eric. Of course he would be here, too. I'd never felt so simultaneously happy and sad to see someone. He spotted me at the same moment, and it was like transmitting thoughts back and forth without words.

He walked over to me.

"We have to make this stop. Somehow."

I nodded. "I have an idea. A way to put some pressure on."

The next morning in the newsroom, I told Ned I thought it was time for me to write the first installment of the mill fire investigation story.

He grinned. "Funny, I was starting to think the same thing. It's time to poke the bear with a stick. Make something happen. But let's look at what you have confirmed so far that we could run with. Do we have enough?"

"I have quotes from the four men who saw suspicious activity the night before the fires. I have the names of the corporate owners and officers of the mills, and Bob and I have finished calling all of them. Total stonewall. They all refused to discuss the fires or comment specifically about the possibility of inventory being moved in just before the fires."

Ned's eyes narrowed. "That might be enough for a first piece. But let's have you and Bob make some calls today and get some officials on the record about this inventory angle. Try Councilwoman Boucher and Councilman Silva—they were on the side of the residents during that council meeting."

"Right, and maybe Bob can call Moreno for a quote, and I can try the state fire marshal."

Ned clapped his hands together. "Good plan. Let's bring this simmering pot to a boil."

We gathered all the comments that day and I worked into the night writing the story. It ran the next day, under the headline: *Eyewitnesses saw unusual activity at four mills before fires.*

Both Boucher and Silva went on the record renewing the call for a special task force to investigate the fires. The state fire marshal said the reported eyewitness accounts, "if credible, would be pertinent to our ongoing open investigations of these matters," but declined to say whether they would actively pursue those witnesses.

Eric provided a quote that corroborated hearing the four witness accounts. "People who are on the fringes of our society are still people. They have eyes and ears. Their voices deserve to be heard, and our public officials have no right to discount them."

Moreno's quote was the most combative:

"These supposed eyewitness accounts that the *Times* has gathered from unreliable vagrants reflect the worst kind of irresponsible journalism. This is a time for our community to come together, not be distracted by ghost stories that an ambitious reporter has fabricated in order to sell papers."

Ned roared when he saw that quote as he was editing the story.

91

"I love when they accuse us of making things up!" he shouted across the newsroom. "That's the telltale comeback line of the guilty."

The day that story rolled off the press marked the beginning of a series of events that could not be stopped, like a boulder pushed off the side of a cliff. I would come to wish, even pray, that I could have altered its course somehow, minimized the wreckage, but there was nothing to be done.

When I arrived at the police station the next morning to do the blotter, the change was obvious immediately. I expected that the cops would be irked by the story, maybe even give me a cold shoulder. But this was intense, personal.

No greeting at all from Teddy as I approached the desk. No basket of reports sitting on the counter. I asked him for them.

"You'll have to wait. We're tied up right now." He never looked up.

I sat down on one of the wooden chairs along the wall. Ten minutes. Twenty.

Finally the basket appeared on the counter with a bang. As I went over and reached for it Teddy's hand held firmly to the other end.

"You'll have to read them and take notes here from now on. In front of me."

That evening, Francie called me over with an urgent wave of her hand as I started to head upstairs to my apartment.

"The cops and firemen are really on the warpath about you," she said in a low voice, even though there was no one else around. "Lonnie said Battalion Chief Nunes was cursing you out at the firehouse last night. Said nobody should give you any information or even talk to you anymore."

"What did Lonnie think?" I'd talked to him a couple of times when Francie had me over for dinner or a cook-out. Friendly guy with a thick mustache and a big laugh.

Francie glanced around and ushered me inside her living room before she answered.

"Lonnie thinks you should keep doing what you're doing. That's what he told me to tell you."

I was dumbfounded.

"Did he say anything else?"

She paused and sucked in a breath. "He said that Nunes has a group of guys around him. Three or four firemen. It's like his clique. He always makes up the schedule so they're all on duty together. That's all he said. I don't know what it means."

That night I found myself thinking back to my memories from the Watergate years. Maybe it was the visit with Dad that stirred up old thoughts, the way the ocean waves churn the sand and bring forth broken bits of shell long buried.

I was seventeen when the televised Senate committee hearings began in 1973 but I'd already been following every crumb of the story since the first reports of the burglary the year before. We didn't get the *Washington Post*, but when our *TIME* magazine arrived in the mail each week I would grab it first, scouring the pages for each new puzzle piece.

I watched every hour of hearings that I could, sitting cross-legged in front of our old Zenith, shouting updates to Dad as he worked in his office. The thing that struck me most deeply through it all were the moments when one of the Republican senators would offer a comment or question that showed they were just as determined as their Democratic colleagues to find the truth about this Republican president. That gave me a sense of calm, and pride, too, knowing that this wouldn't be a whitewash, that we would get to the bottom of it and our country would be fine.

I still believed there will always be good people with the guts to stand up and do the right thing. I thought about what Lonnie had told Francie. He was taking a risk. I had to think it was because he was one of the good guys. Something was not setting quite right with him, perhaps. I thought about what Ned had said weeks earlier. Digging into public records was only going to take us so far. I needed to find some sources on the inside. Maybe Lonnie could be one.

A few days later, I came home from work to find the flag up on my small mailbox on the pole next to Francie's. Probably a note or clipping from Dad. I parked and walked back to the curb to see what was inside.

It was a plain white business envelope. As I reached for it I noticed there was no stamp or postmark and my heartbeat quickened. On the outside my name was typed and under it, the word CONFIDENTIAL.

I took it up to my apartment and set it on the dining room table. So many thoughts ran through my mind. Could it be a threat? Something meant to scare me?

I ripped it open and withdrew a single piece of paper. On it was typewritten:

You are on the right track, but you need to think bigger.
The fires are just one piece.
Ask for the itemized list of losses filed by each owner after each fire.
And remember that a car wash can be a high-volume, mainly cash business.
I will try to help you where I can.

I knew that Ned and Bob were still at the paper, working on a special supplement on the town election coming up in November. I raced over with the letter.

Ned let out a low whistle as he read it, then handed it to Bob.

"I think you've found your Deep Throat. Any idea who it might be?" Ned asked.

I shook my head. "Not really. There's a fireman—a friend of a friend—who passed along some advice the other day. But somehow, this doesn't sound like him. The tone of it..."

"Sounds like somebody at a higher level," said Bob.

"And somebody trying to point me in the right direction without risking exposure," I said. "What do you think the car wash comment means?"

Something seemed to click in Bob's mind.

"Hmmm, very interesting. Moreno owns a string of car washes called Blue Wave. They sit on the same property as his dealerships."

He paused, his brow crinkled.

"I remember seeing something about his car washes in the business transaction legal notices in the paper a while back. Probably within the last year. I'll spend some time in the archives and see if I can pull it up."

"And I'll check out the tip about the lists of inventory losses," I said.

Ned looked pleased. He leaned back in his chair, hands laced together behind his head.

"Ladies and gentlemen, the dam is starting to break."

94

I had trouble sleeping that night. There was something vaguely creepy about the use of my mailbox to deliver the note. Assuming it was someone other than Lonnie that meant my secret source must have followed me home at some point. I pictured a shadowy figure— a man, I guessed—his cap pulled down to conceal his face, following just far enough behind me to avoid suspicion, like a scene out of a TV cop show.

Maybe he watched from a distance as I exited my car, checked the mailbox and then headed up the stairs to my apartment. Did he wait there, parked somewhere out of sight, until the house went dark and silent? Did he worry about being seen as he quietly pulled the mailbox door open and slid the envelope inside? Must have thought something important was at stake. And, just possibly, that he had enough clout to explain his way out of any questions if someone spotted him.

As a reporter I've been trained to strive for objectivity, so I also had to entertain the idea that this person may have an entirely different motive. It was possible the information was meant to purposely throw me off track and lead my investigation astray, perhaps to buy time. Given the kind of specific details in the note however, I was still more confident he was trying to guide me rather than send me on a wild goose chase around town.

I rolled over on my back and stared up at the popcorn ceiling. I didn't like this feeling of being passive; waiting for the next message. This should be a two-way conversation.

I decided to trust my instincts and leave a note for him. I would place it inside the mailbox each night when I got home and remove it each morning (so the mailman wouldn't think I was a lunatic). At some point, I assumed, he would return with another message and find mine. I wrote:

Can you tell me who you are? You have my word I will never reveal your identity to anyone.
Can we meet somewhere?
Is there one person behind all of the fires?

I waited. Meanwhile, Bob and I chased down clues from the first note.

At the police station, I asked Teddy for the lists of lost inventory from all of the fires.

95

He didn't look up from his desk.

"Those aren't part of the public record," he said.

"But they're part of the official police report of a fire, as I understand it," I countered.

"Talk to Lieutenant Pelletier." He looked up, his gaze cold as a statue. "You ain't getting them from me."

Over at Detective Division, I found Pelletier leafing through a file cabinet in the back.

"Miss Sullivan! You've come to brighten our day."

I explained what I was after. He shook his head.

"Teddy's right. We don't share that information. That would violate the rights of the property owner. They're just providing that information to us to document their losses so they can submit the claim to their insurance company. There's no public interest to be served in giving you somebody's private business information."

I wasn't about to let it go.

"OK. We're probably going to file a formal request. Just to make sure. I'll get back to you."

Pelletier chuckled in a way that I found particularly condescending.

"Miss Sullivan, did anyone ever tell you that you're like a dog with a bone?"

Back in the newsroom, I conferred with Ned on our next step. While I was at Oakmont, just after the Watergate upheaval, Congress put more teeth in the Freedom of Information Act to make it easier to expose government wrongdoing. I thought this might be my first chance to use it.

"This sounds like it's worth filing a FOIA request," Ned agreed. "Let's give it a shot." He paused. "I'll have to run it by Ruskin, but I think he'll be on board."

Just then I saw Bob walking toward us from across the newsroom, holding up a yellowed newspaper.

"Eureka!" he shouted, prompting heads around the room to turn and look up. He brought the paper over to Ned's desk and opened it to the page of legal notices. He traced with his finger down a long column of business transactions, stopping at this item, dated a year earlier:

Blue Wave Car Wash, Inc., conveyed to RD Holdings, LLC.

He tapped his finger on the name at the end of the notice.

"That's one of Roland Ducharme's companies. From the notice, it sounds like Ducharme took over the majority ownership in a partnership with Moreno.

Ned and I exchanged looks. This was far from a smoking gun, nothing conclusive. But it finally gave me a connection between Moreno and Ducharme that I could pursue.

"Nice piece of digging," I said to Bob. "I think we need to make some updates to our wall upstairs."

The next morning, after a series of closed-door meetings in Ruskin's office, Ned emerged and gave me a thumbs-up from across the newsroom. The paper's attorney filed the FOIA request with the West Wicklow Police Department that afternoon, and I wrote a story about it in the next day's paper. Ruskin even wrote an editorial explaining why it was important for us to do everything we could to get to the bottom of the mill fire epidemic. I had to admit, it was fairly hard-hitting for a Ruskin editorial. *Since the Town Council has declined to act, we have a responsibility to keep trying to find the truth.*

Later that day, Ruskin stopped by my desk. I was surprised. I hadn't exchanged more than a few sentences with him since I came to the paper. He was somewhat of a ghost-like presence, slipping in and out with little notice except for the periodic tapping sounds emanating from his typewriter in the corner as he wrote an editorial or column.

"Good work, Meg," he said. He appeared to want to say something more, but just kept nodding and slapping his rolled-up newspaper against the palm of his hand. Finally, he said, "Keep it up!" and walked off.

I liked to think that the work we were doing had rekindled something in Ruskin, a passion for the family newspaper business that he might have had as a young man, then lost along the way. Something that made him stop worrying about losing advertisers or offending powerful people in town. Maybe Ned was having a good influence on him.

When I got home at the end of that week I found another message in my mailbox. Inside the envelope were two pieces of paper. The first said:

Good move on the FOIA request. Keep the pressure on.

Remember that in business, the people who handle the books are very important.

Be careful.

The second paper was my note to him. In black pen, he had printed a single letter to indicate his yes or no to each question.

Would he tell me his name? **N**

Could we meet? **N**

My heart started to race as I saw the last line:

Is there one person behind all of the fires?

Y.

Chapter Ten

Up until this point, the mill fires had been strictly local news. But when we ran the story on our FOIA request, the UPI wire picked it up. We heard that it ran in papers around the state and even made the "Around New England" briefs in a few big city dailies in Connecticut and Massachusetts.

That gave me an idea. I'd been trying to figure out a way to get to Ducharme. Of course, I had absolutely nothing on him. I lectured myself that I needed to remain objective and not get ahead of the facts. But the fires drawing attention around the region could potentially be a concern for local business leaders. It could hurt the economy, make people reluctant to live, work and invest here.

I decided to do a story from that angle, interviewing major business figures in town to get their perspective. And who better to include in that group than Roland Ducharme, the man whose business interests were laced throughout West Wicklow like a spider's web?

On a cold November morning after deadline, I walked to the small building on Main where Ducharme had his office. A chill had seeped into the town and just a few brown leaves clung to the tree branches, shuddering with each blast of wind. It was that same bone-chilling wind I'd felt as I walked to the spot on the sidewalk where John Harrington lay. The same fear, too. *Steady*, I told myself. *You can do this.* I entered through the front door and climbed the stone steps to the second floor, my footfalls echoing through the empty space.

At the end of the hall I found the door to Suite 201, the address Bob had given me. There was no business name etched on the frosted glass panel, just the suite number. Through the wavy glass I could see lights on inside and the distorted shape of a head bending down at a desk.

I turned the brass knob and stepped inside.

A young woman at the reception desk looked up at me with the blank innocence of a baby. She was striking, early twenties, with shiny blonde hair that fell simply to her shoulders.

"May I help you?"

I introduced myself and saw a flicker of recognition combined with wariness cross her face.

"Yes, I've seen your name. My mother gets the *Times*."

I said I was hoping I might arrange a brief interview with Mr. Ducharme.

"I'm sorry, he's not in at the moment." She clipped her words as though reading from a script. "If you tell me what it's about, I can give him the message when he gets back."

I explained the focus of the piece I was working on. "With Mr. Ducharme being the leading businessman in the community, I thought it would be important to get his perspective," I said. "People in town look up to him."

Her expression softened.

"Oh, yes," she said. "He's an amazing person. I've never met anyone as smart as him."

There was a straight chair next to her desk and I slid casually into it.

"I bet he is. I've heard about all his success."

She leaned toward me. "That's just America for you, isn't it?" she said. "If you're smart and work hard, there's no stopping you. That's what Mr. Ducharme always says."

She reached for her pink message pad and wrote down my name and number.

"You know," she said, "these fires are so horrible. I actually know one of the girls you interviewed. Darlene Silva. We were in the same class in high school."

We talked for a few minutes about Darlene, Petey and the Estrella restaurant.

"What's your name?" I asked. "The next time I see Darlene I'll tell her you said hello."

She blushed. "I'm sorry—I should have introduced myself." She extended her hand. "I'm Joan Levesque."

She glanced over at her typewriter. "Well, I suppose I should get back to my letters."

"Of course. I don't want to hold you up." I started to rise from the chair but then she kept talking and I eased myself slowly back down.

100

"Actually I've always been curious about reporters," she said, twisting the end of her hair around her finger. "That must be a really interesting job."

I told her a little about the work, and how I'd wanted to do this since I was a young girl. "Every day is something new. I like talking to people, hearing their stories."

"And you're good at it!" she said. "Look at me, rambling on."

She explained that she'd attended secretarial school after graduating from West Wicklow High. "But I'm really more than a secretary here. My mom was a bookkeeper and she taught me a lot. So I help Mr. Ducharme with the books, too."

That word rang in my ears like an alarm. *Books.*

"Wow, that must be complicated," I said. "I understand he has a lot of businesses."

"Oh, you have no idea!"

Just then, out of the corner of my eye, I saw a shadow cross the frosted glass door panel. The doorknob turned.

"Mr. Ducharme!" Joan looked flustered.

A tall man in a black suit with salt and pepper hair glowered down at me. He appeared to be in his mid-forties, attractive in the way older, powerful men often are: well-coiffed and well-dressed, with an air of confidence even stronger than his cologne.

I popped up from my chair. "Mr. Ducharme, I'm Meg Sullivan from the *Times*. I'm working on a story…"

Joan interjected. "She wants to interview leading businessmen in town about the fires."

He glared at her, unblinking, standing motionless except for a slight twitch of his jaw. He appeared to be a bomb in human form, ticking down to an explosion.

But instead he turned and smiled at me. A practiced smile, like that of a car salesman.

"I'm sorry. That won't be possible. I don't do interviews."

I persisted. "I was wondering if you think this problem with the mill fires will hurt the town's image as a place to invest and build businesses. You've been so successful here. I think readers would really value your opinion."

He was silent for a moment. His jaw continued to twitch, and then there came a flash across his face as though he had methodically processed this unexpected situation and once again felt supremely in control.

"I think West Wicklow will be just fine once the media stops all of this hysteria."

With that, he swung open the door and pointed the way out.

"Have a nice day, Miss Sullivan."

The glass rattled in the doorframe as he slammed it behind me.

Fumbling to put my notebook in my bag, I realized I was shaking. I'd thought getting a chance to talk to Ducharme would be a big achievement but, as it turned out, the most momentous thing that happened was meeting Joan. As someone had told me recently, the people who handle the books are very important.

The story ran the next day, featuring quotes from the head of the local bank, a jeweler on Main, the developer of a new industrial park out by the interstate, and a half-dozen other prominent businessmen. Tried but couldn't find any prominent women business leaders. You've come a long way, baby.

All of those quoted said they were concerned about the impact on the town's business climate, as well as the human impact on the fire victims. At the end of the piece I included the quote from Ducharme. Although he said he didn't do interviews, I had identified myself as a reporter, so what he said after that was fair game. Still, it felt unsettling to see his name in print when I pulled a copy of the paper from the production room as I headed out to lunch. I remembered the expression on his face when he heard who I was and why I was there.

During those weeks in November, the whole newsroom staff seemed to shift into a higher gear. As Bob and I kept working the fire investigation, John broke a hot story about the Cheshire School Board holding a secret meeting to plan budget cuts that would include dropping high school sports. His piece prompted parents to picket the school administration building until they held another public meeting to debate—and eventually scale back—the cuts.

Maddie, too, was mixing in more serious features along with her required weekend fluff stories on parades and 100th birthdays. She came by my desk one afternoon when it was just the two of us in the newsroom.

"I have an idea for an investigative story but I'm not sure how to go about it," she said, pulling up a chair. She told me she'd covered a good-news piece the week before about the local child welfare agency finding a family willing to adopt a teen in foster care.

"When I stopped by the foster home to snap a few photos to go with the story, something didn't seem right," she said. "There were kids running around everywhere. I know the houses on that street and they've only got two bedrooms. There was a folded-up blanket and pillow on the couch in the living room, like somebody was sleeping there. I asked the teen who was being adopted how many kids lived in the home and he said maybe six or seven. But I don't know where to take it from here."

I had to smile. *What's wrong with this picture?* Maddie had spotted something. She had good instincts. I gave her some ideas for next steps. To ask the local agency for the number of foster kids in its system, and the number of licensed foster care beds. And find out the regulations under state law for foster home capacity.

"You know," she said, "I never would have been looking for a story like this before you came here." She laughed. "So, I guess girls can do this kind of Woodward-and-Bernstein thing."

"Damn right we can," I said.

Two weeks later, Maddie's story on overcrowding in area foster homes raised a furor and prompted the state child welfare department to intervene. Shortly after that, at our reporter meeting after deadline one day, Ned told us he had something to say before each of us gave our updates.

"I want to tell you about a call I got yesterday afternoon."

We all shifted in our seats. What was this about?

"The call was from a woman named Nancy Mason," he began. "She described herself as just a normal mom and subscriber. And then she said, 'I want to tell you that I've noticed over the last few months that you've been doing some really hard-hitting stories, holding the powers-that-be accountable. I know you probably don't get a lot of praise, but I wanted you to know that there are people out there like me who appreciate what you're doing.'"

We all exchanged looks of disbelief.

"I know," Ned said. "In my whole career, I've never received a call like that." He looked around the circle at us. "That's because of the good work by every single one of you. Good reporting. Good writing."

He paused. "And one more thing. I've worked for bigger papers in bigger cities. But none better."

That Saturday night, Joel and Sara had a big party with friends and neighbors to celebrate Joel's birthday. As I walked through the door and looked around, I saw all of the familiar faces from the newsroom plus one more: Eric.

It had been several weeks since I'd seen him, weeks that I'd spent trying not to think about him while at the same time hoping desperately to bump into him everywhere I went. It was exhausting. But sometimes I would think of that day on the beach and be filled with a slowed-down, languid feeling, like the way honey falls from a teaspoon, such slow sweetness.

He saw me and worked his way across the crowded room, squeezing through openings between clutches of chattering guests.

"It was nice of Joel to invite me," he said, as if to explain his presence.

I nodded. "I know the two of you have worked a lot of fires together." I tried not to look directly into his eyes, gazing off toward the corner where Joel was talking with the newsroom gang.

"He's one fierce photographer," Eric said. "I've never seen anyone run toward danger like that."

This was a strange sensation, chit-chatting with someone so coolly while your insides were boiling. I had to break away.

"I better go add this to the BYOB table," I said, holding up my standard bottle of rosé.

"Sure," he said.

Did his voice sound forlorn? Or was that just me?

He called after me.

"Let me walk you to your car, later. Okay?"

I glanced back over my shoulder and nodded, then walked away, half of me wanting to scurry back, the other half just wanting to disappear.

I spent the next couple of hours constantly aware of his presence, my eyes darting around, trying to stay occupied in other conversations.

"Are you okay?" Sara said to me at one point when we were talking in a quiet corner. "You seem as nervous as a cat."

By midnight, everyone was dancing. Sara had rolled up the rug in the living room, dimmed the lights and cranked up the stereo. Joel was picking the music, working his way backward in their record collection to favorites from our college years. Now it was Rod Stewart's *Every Picture Tells a Story* driving everyone into a euphoric state. Nobody dancing with anyone in particular, just hopping and swaying in a frenzy, mouthing the words: *Every picture tells a story, don't it?* Louder and more crazed with each repetition:

Every picture tells a story, DON'T IT?

For an instant, Eric's orbit intersected with mine. I envied the way he danced, unselfconscious and free. For those few seconds, it felt like we were a couple. Then the music ended and we found ourselves standing awkwardly close to each other. Over his shoulder, I saw Sara smile at me knowingly.

Time to go. I was worn out. I looked at Eric, his face still flushed from dancing, and motioned with my head toward the door.

For a second, he looked crestfallen, then seemed to catch himself.

"May I escort you to your motor carriage, miss," he said in a mock-British, Monty Python voice.

"Oh, that would be lovely," I replied in the same voice.

We said our goodbyes and headed outside.

"I'm parked at the end of the block," I said. We began to walk down the hill. The air was cold and dry, and above us the stars crowded a black sky. All was silent except for our footsteps.

"It's nice of you to walk me," I said, trying to fill the void.

He smiled. "I wouldn't want anything to happen to you." He paused. "It was really good to see you, Meg."

I stopped, frozen in place.

"What is it?" he asked.

"My car," I said, pointing to the Hornet. It sat lower than normal, looking wounded. We both started to circle it. All four tires were flat.

"My God," Eric said, kneeling down to look closely at one of the back tires, rubbing his hand along the rubber. His face turned ashen as he looked up at me.

"They've been slashed."

That night felt like it would never end. We went back to Joel's to call the police. The newsroom gang circled me like family members around a hospital bed. Worried expressions all around. A hand on my shoulder. A hug.

I didn't recognize the officer who responded. He examined the tires and took a report.

"Have you had a dispute of any kind, any bad blood with anyone?" he asked me.

"Not really," I replied.

Joel, standing behind me, interjected. "She's a reporter for the *Times*."

"Yeah, I recognized the name," the officer said. "Look, miss, I wouldn't read too much into this. Could just have been kids, drunk, wanting to cause trouble."

I nodded. By then the tow truck had come for the car.

"I'll give you a ride home," Eric said.

On the way, I had trouble organizing my thoughts. It occurred to me that pulling up to my apartment at three in the morning, Francie would probably be celebrating that something finally happened in my love life. I wondered whether I should be afraid. I decided instead to think of this as the work of some juvenile delinquents.

Eric must have read my thoughts.

"You know," he began, "I don't think it's a coincidence that this happened a few days after you put Ducharme's name in the paper for the first time."

I slumped back in my seat.

"You're right. I've been trying to see this as something random, but the most likely explanation is that this was a message."

We had reached my driveway. A low light shone from Francie's upstairs window. The curtain moved. The light went out.

As I started to get out, Eric reached over and squeezed my upper arm gently.

"Please be careful."

Chapter Eleven

The next week passed without anything strange happening. My work on the mill fire investigation was on hold as we waited to hear a decision on our FOIA request, which was now in the courts.

One day, after deadline, I stopped at the post office on Main to mail a batch of past issues of the paper to Dad. He called it his "care package." I sent one every couple of weeks so he could keep up with what was happening in town.

Inside the vestibule, the wall to my right was lined with rows of post office boxes. At the far end, I saw Joan from Ducharme's office opening the door to one of the boxes and scooping the contents into a plastic bin.

She was so intent on her work that she didn't look my way. I was ready to open the glass door to go inside when she pulled another key from her pocket, examined the tag on it, then inserted it in the box below the one she'd just emptied. She reached inside and pulled a few more envelopes into the bin.

I tried to remain still and unobtrusive as she continued her work. Other people came and went through the lobby doors, helping me feel less conspicuous. I fingered the large manila envelope in my hand, figuring that at any moment, if she looked my way I could continue toward the door.

By my count, she opened and emptied fourteen boxes in all, dropping down onto her haunches to get at the lower ones. She snapped the fourteenth door closed and turned toward me just as a tall, burly man exited through the glass door and I ducked inside, using him for cover. My heart started pounding, which annoyed me. Just going to mail an innocent package, after all. I stood in line with my back to the door.

When I came back through the vestibule I returned to the spot where she had stood and I pulled out my notebook. I couldn't be exactly sure which boxes she had opened but I had a good idea. I tried to visualize her in my mind, copying down the box numbers in the last two columns in the corner, from top to bottom.

Afterward, I walked quickly back to the paper and sprinted up the steps to the war room. I grabbed a red felt pen. The first P.O. box in my notebook was 424. I scanned the list on the wall of the P.O. box addresses for the owners of the fourteen mills that had gone up in flames, including the most recent fire at Valley.

No number 424. No 423 or 422.

I am an idiot.

Then, I spotted a 425 in my book and again on the wall, listed as the box number for CM Associates, owner of the Century Mill. Circled it in red.

I am perhaps not a total idiot.

In all, I circled eight matches of P.O. box numbers to the list of mill owners.

I sat down on the chair and took a deep breath. This was certainly not anything solid enough to publish. Maybe at some point, it would sync up to something meaningful. But for now, it gave me some confidence that I was on the right track in linking Ducharme to the fires.

The week before Thanksgiving, we got word that a county judge had ordered the town to comply with our FOIA request, overruling the town solicitor's decision to withhold the documents. Under court order, a large box of records was delivered to the newsroom as Joel snapped photos.

"This is our top priority," Ned said. "All hands on deck."

We divided the fourteen sets of records among me, Bob, John and Maddie. After we took notes on what we found in each set, we passed it on to Rosie, who had been pulled into service to type up a full list of all goods claimed as lost in the fires.

"I want to print the entire list," Ned said. "Let's get it all out there."

Through that afternoon and into the evening, we worked. Ruskin walked through and gave us a pep talk. Ned ordered pizza.

As we ate, we compared notes on what we were finding. In every fire, long lists of expensive goods were claimed as inventory lost. Gloria Vanderbilt jeans. Gucci hobo bags. Mink stoles and leather jackets.

"At each fire, they're claiming that hundreds of boxes of inventory were totally incinerated," Bob said. "And that does match up with the wording in the fire marshal's reports that significant inventory was lost in each of the fires."

"And yet," I said, "the guys we interviewed who were in those mills said all they saw were a few pallets of boxes, some of which were filled with junk."

Ned interrupted. "We're going to need a couple of other sources—ones whose credibility can't be attacked so easily."

I thought about the piece of information that Francie's boyfriend, Lonnie, had passed along to me. That Battalion Chief Nunes had a regular crew of firemen who worked together. Maybe Lonnie could help me get the sources I needed.

"I've got an angle I want to work on," I told the group. "Can we get a copy of Rosie's list? I want to take it with me."

Ned nodded. "She's just typing up the last one now. Let me run it through the scanner to get it into my computer, and then you can have it." He paused. "What's your angle?"

"Not completely sure. But there's somebody in the fire department who's been a little bit supportive in the past. Let me work on it."

Joel had been sorting prints on the counter and looked up.

"I've got some friends over there too. There's one I'm thinking of who's close enough where I could test the waters and see if they might be inclined to talk."

With Francie's help, Lonnie agreed to talk to me with the promise he wouldn't be named. It was a blustery night, the first real blast of winter weather. Francie lit the kerosene heater in her living room to take the extra chill off. I sat next to Lonnie on the couch, laying the lists of inventory on the coffee table.

He read through each one. A couple of times, he snorted and shook his head as he traced his finger down the list.

"So, what do you think?" I asked when he finished.

He leaned back against the sofa.

"I wasn't at every one of these fires. But for the ones where I was there, I can tell you that these lists are total bullshit."

The more we talked, the angrier he grew.

"Some dirty bastards are getting rich while guys like us are putting our lives on the line," he said. "If it takes somebody like me talking to somebody like you to expose it, then so be it."

For the rest of that week and into the weekend, we worked on putting the story together. Joel's friend, a young fireman named Scott who had joined the department about a year ago, agreed to talk with me under the same terms Lonnie had: on the record, but not for attribution by name. We met in Joel's kitchen. He corroborated Lonnie's assessment: the volume and type of inventory on the lists did not match what he saw at the fire scenes.

Ned was intent on publishing the story before Thanksgiving break. I worked late into the evening Monday and by noon on Tuesday the paper rolled off the presses with the blaring headline: *Claims of Lost Inventory in Mill Fires Exaggerated, Sources Reveal.*

In the story, I described my two sources as "town employees with first-hand knowledge of the fire scenes." I also quoted a spokesperson in the state Department of Insurance, who said that "whenever information is brought to our attention that indicates the possibility of fraud, we pursue it vigorously with appropriate law enforcement agencies."

By that afternoon, the newsroom was a frenzy of ringing phones. Ruskin took calls from the town solicitor, who complained about the use of unnamed sources, and from Moreno, who threatened to pull all of his car dealership and car wash advertising unless the *Times* stopped its "sensationalized and false reporting."

Meanwhile, Bob worked on a reaction story for the next day's paper. Council members Boucher and Silva called again for an independent investigation into all aspects of the mill fires.

I felt like I had started to push a snowball down a hill and it was turning into an avalanche. I wasn't sure which way the story would go from here. And in the back of my mind, I kept remembering my Hornet with its tires slashed. I had started being more aware of my surroundings after that. Just simple things, like checking to see if I was being followed and glancing over my shoulder when leaving the paper late at night.

Part of me was glad for the holiday coming to give us all a chance to catch our breath. I had made plans to drive down to the Jersey shore after deadline on Wednesday to spend the long weekend with my Dad at the family cottage in Cape May. We'd been going there every summer as long as I could remember. Even in the winter, we liked to spend time there, taking brisk walks along the shore and lighting a fire at night in the woodstove.

Early Wednesday morning, I got in my car and headed toward town. I was running late for my early police blotter work and was on automatic pilot as I slipped the car into gear and turned left to go down the hill.

As I started to pick up speed, I unconsciously moved my foot from the accelerator and started to lightly push the brake pedal.

My foot went straight to the floor. It was as though there was no resistance at all.

No brakes.

My speed increased. I knew this hill. No flat stretches, no ups and downs. Just a continuous pitch downward to the bottom of the Valley. Options raced through my mind. *Use the handbrake.* I remembered my Dad telling me that once. I applied it but it barely slowed me down.

Think. Think! My mind was cluttered with thoughts. Who did this? Why hadn't I been more careful? I swept them all away. *Think!* Suddenly I remembered the runaway truck ramps on the Pennsylvania Turnpike. As a kid I always thought that was funny. I used to imagine the trucks, cartoon-like, speeding up the grassy ramp. Now, I tried to remember what was ahead. Around the next curve on the left was the country club. I saw the gently rolling mounds of manicured grass coming up at me and quickly yanked the wheel over to the left, bounding across the golf cart trail, into a fairway and finally coming to rest on top of the raised green of the sixteenth hole.

I sat there, shaking, with both hands still gripping the wheel. The view through my windshield looked so oddly tranquil. A crow flew by and landed on the bare branch of a nearby tree. Not a human soul anywhere in sight. I was almost killed. Is that how quickly it can happen? Or not happen? The random chance of a turn in the road, the time it takes for a bird to flap its wings. Out of the corner of my eye I could see a caretaker from the club rumbling toward me in a cart. He took me to the clubhouse and he called the police while I sat at the club manager's desk and called Ned's line on a shiny black rotary phone, my fingers barely steady enough to move the dialer.

Both Ned and Ruskin insisted that we a run a story about what happened. They brought Bob with them to interview me once the police were finished taking my statement. Investigators checked the car and found that the brake line had been cut.

Through all of the coming and going, Ned sat with me.

111

"This is getting way too dangerous," he said. He fumbled for the pack of cigarettes in his chest pocket and lit one with shaky fingers.

I felt like I was the one who needed to reassure him.

"If I can get the car fixed today I can still make it to Jersey for Thanksgiving," I said. "It will put a little distance between me and…" I struggled for the words. "Between me and whatever the hell this is."

Ned had a look in his eyes I'd never seen. The way someone wading in the ocean looks at that moment when a rogue wave knocks them off their feet, the undertow yanking away what they assumed was a solid place to stand.

I felt that same way. Upended. Like anything might happen next.

Francie had a friend who was a mechanic. I arranged for my car to be towed to his garage, and he had the brakes repaired by late afternoon. When I returned to the apartment with the car, she had cleaned out the other half of her garage so I could park the Hornet in there alongside hers, safe from potential evildoers.

"Are you sure you're okay?" she asked, looking at me intently. "Whoever did this is some kind of psychopath. I hope the cops are going to do something about it."

"I'm fine, really." I lied pretty well, I thought. "Just going to hang out the rest of the evening and then I'll get an early start in the morning."

She nodded grudgingly as I climbed the stairs to my place.

Once I closed and locked the door behind me, all the strength drained out and I felt like my legs might not support me. I was filled with a searing awareness of the fragility of my own life. I was alive, but I could just as easily have died today. I could not seem to calm myself down.

I thought back to the night at the Festa when Moreno handed me that card. Maybe I should have called the number. Maybe I still could. I felt like people were arguing inside my head, but it was all me. Sure, I liked being a reporter. This was my dream. But was it worth dying for? How idiotic and pointless seemed my little investigation. Pathetic, even. Fires in a small town. My "war room." Meaningless markings on a wall.

I went to my bedroom and opened the little jewelry box that I'd brought with me from my dorm room. I pried up the red felt panel inside and pulled out a wrinkled joint hidden below. I'd kept a stash of them there during college and brought this one with me in the move. I wasn't sure why. Something about wanting to stay just a little bit rebellious.

I found a pack of matches in the kitchen drawer, propped myself up on the sofa and lit up. Who cared, at this point, whether Francie might find out? Who cared if the cops burst in, tipped off by whatever creep was behind this? Any scenario—arrest, being publicly discredited, losing my job—seemed less dire than my current circumstances, and thus, foolish to worry about. At first, the joint did nothing to calm the wild thing running around in my chest. But after a time spent drawing in and out, letting myself be enveloped by its mossy smell, I could feel parts unspooling inside me and an ease flowing through my veins.

At that point I remembered that marijuana can also bring paranoia, and I wished I had reached for the rosé in the refrigerator instead. *You're not paranoid if people really are out to get you.* That made me laugh, albeit wryly. Still, I listened for sounds outside. Twice I hopped up to peep out the curtain.

Then I heard the sound of a car in Francie's driveway and looked out.

It was Eric's Jeep.

When I opened the door, neither of us spoke. He came inside and, in the instant after I'd turned the lock, drew me close.

"Joel called me," he said, then held me tighter.

As we walked to the couch, he glanced at the glowing joint in the ashtray but said nothing. He picked it up, took a hit, and passed it to me.

I inhaled deeply. "I'm all messed up." My voice didn't sound like me.

We sat there for a time, until we could no longer hold the joint without burning our fingers.

"We've been fools," he said.

I nodded. "Very noble, excruciatingly ethical fools."

When he leaned over to kiss me, I knew that this time, I was fresh out of reasons to stop.

Chapter Twelve

By eight the next morning, I crossed the Rhode Island border into Connecticut, heading south on I-95. Eric had left just before daybreak so I could get an early start. He tried and failed to convince me to stay.

I probably wasn't in the best shape for a six-hour road trip, but hell, I had survived driving a car with no brakes. My eyes had been opened to a new and reckless way of seeing the world.

I still didn't know what to think about the events of the last twenty-four hours. I'd called Dad from the country club a few hours after the crash but couldn't bring myself to tell him over the phone. I said something at work had delayed me, but I would still be there for Thanksgiving.

"Your voice sounds funny," he said. "Are you getting a cold?" He made a joke about me arriving late so I wouldn't have to help him cook the dinner.

"And by the way, we're setting another place at the table," he said. "Eveline is going to join us."

A wave of disappointment shot through me. I wanted it to be just me and him. I wanted to finally tell him everything. Maybe he could help settle those arguments I was having inside my head.

Now, as the woodsy Connecticut scenery swept by, the possible choices started firing at one another again.

I could get a job at another paper. Something in Rhode Island or near enough that I could still see Eric. The thought of him was like one calm spot in a raging ocean. Any scenario would have to include him now. Non-negotiable. But how would I explain to a prospective employer why I was leaving a job after only three months? *Somebody tried to kill me, but don't worry, I'll just write fluff stories at your paper!* Or I could get out of journalism entirely. That scenario gave me a feeling like somebody died. Still, it was an option. Dad had always said he would pay my way through law school if that's what I wanted.

Nothing made any sense to me. Maybe once I got to Cape May, things would be clearer. I did notice that when I got out of the car to get gas, miles and miles away from West Wicklow, the fearfulness had dropped from my shoulders. I hadn't realized until that moment just how heavy it had been to carry. Now, at a rest stop on the Garden State Parkway, I didn't have to check to see who might be lurking behind the gas pump. I could finally breathe easily.

Cape May was like a charming old friend of the family, one who still looked fabulous wearing her hair the same way she had in her youth. Gracious Victorian hotels and cottages arrayed in crisp paint and bric-a-brac marched to the Atlantic along every street. My summer childhood memories were all set in Cape May, in the earliest years with Mom holding my hand at the water's edge to jump the waves, and then later with Dad, aunts and uncles, cousins and summer friends who spent time at our cottage.

It was a tidy bungalow, painted a certain blue that reminded me of the salt marsh channels in the early morning, pale and translucent. As I turned onto our street on this grey and bitter Thanksgiving afternoon I could see the familiar swatch of color at the end of the block, and once again it summoned memories of salty mornings spent crabbing in a little skiff, the dark green handline slippery in my small fingers, Mom's hair tied up in a kerchief, Dad with the net ready to scoop up my catch.

I drove past the grand three-story white Victorian, two houses down from ours. As kids we used to call it "The Wedding Cake." It was the retreat house for the order of nuns who ran Oakmont, and on a fair day in season, the rockers on the wide front porch would be filled with nuns in their white summer veils, laughing and rocking. Now, the porch was empty but lights shone inside through sheer lace curtains. Perhaps Sister had come to visit her old friends, had run into Dad and he invited her to join us. *Eveline*, I corrected myself. Not Sister anymore. Must remember.

When I opened the door, there was Eveline, bending to place a tray of deviled eggs and olives on the coffee table in the living room.

"My goodness! We didn't hear you pull up." Her smile was warm as she scrambled over and hugged me.

"Is that Meg?" Dad's voice boomed from the kitchen and suddenly he was there in front of me in a gravy-splashed apron, wrapping me in his big embrace.

He pulled back to look at me.

"So glad you made it, honey. How was your drive?"

116

"Fine, no problems." I was trying to figure out exactly when I would explain what happened. With Eveline here, the time didn't seem right. Maybe after dinner. I didn't want to spoil everything.

"I made your favorite butternut squash with maple syrup," he said, going back in the kitchen. "The turkey will be out in a half-hour, so get comfortable. Try the deviled eggs that Eveline made. They're amazing."

Eveline blushed. "I'm learning to cook for the first time in my life. It's humbling."

I stowed my jacket and bag in the bedroom and came back to sit next to her on the couch. I tried a deviled egg. A bit mustardy for my taste, but not bad.

"Dad's right, these are great," I said between bites. She looked grateful.

"I know your Dad has told you about my…the change in my circumstances," she said. It was the first time I'd ever seen her look less than totally composed. The regal gaze I remembered from college was gone. Her eyes darted around the room and back to her lap as she smoothed her red wool skirt with the palm of her hands. She sighed. "The elephant in the room, as it were!"

If she only knew. *I brought another elephant with me, and I think mine's even bigger.*

"I'm sure it was a tough decision," I said. I didn't want to pry into anything too personal. "Where are you living now?"

"I'm renting a room from a family in West Philadelphia. Nice people that I'd met years ago in our community work. And I have a job!" She smiled broadly. "I'm doing outreach for a nonprofit focused on lead paint poisoning prevention. Knocking on doors again. Back to my roots."

"And she's causing trouble again, of course," Dad chimed in as he carried the turkey on a platter and set it in the middle of the table. "Tell Meg about the protest."

She blushed again and dismissed him with a wave of her hand. "No, no, I just helped some of the young mothers bring their concerns to the City Council meeting. It's not acceptable! The city is letting landlords rent these apartments with peeling lead paint everywhere. These babies are being literally poisoned."

"Okay, we can talk more about saving the world at the table," Dad said. "Dinner is ready."

We talked and ate for hours. And drank. Dad opened a bottle of Asti Spumanti and poured it into the petite flutes that were a wedding gift and only appeared on New Year's Eve or special occasions. Two hours into the meal he popped a second bottle. We teased Eveline about drinking.

"Well, Jesus turned water into wine, so I think he'd approve," she said, holding up her glass for a refill.

"And you know," she added with a conspiratorial arch of her eyebrows, "nuns do drink. A wee bit of sherry after vespers was not unheard of."

The laughter and conversation spread like a balm over my raw wounds. Maybe it was good that she was here. I could ignore my elephant, for the most part. There were a few questions about how things were going at the paper but I was able to steer away from the latest developments.

Eveline wanted to know what was happening with the men who were sleeping in the mills.

"I have a friend, Eric," I began, and noticed Dad lean in. "He's a community organizer for the Alliance for Social Justice chapter up there. He's been able to find safer shelter for most of them now."

She took a bite of pumpkin pie. "He sounds like a good person."

Now I felt my cheeks burning. "Yes, he's very…passionate about helping people." I heard myself stumble over the word "passionate." I took another sip of Asti.

Dad and Eveline exchanged glances.

"I'm sure he is," she said. "When there's goodness inside a person it flows out and through all things." She paused for a moment and looked squarely at me. "I can't tell you how proud I am of the work you're doing. That one of our graduates is fighting for these people. Fighting for the truth. It's exactly what I prayed for when we started the journalism program. That we could have strong young women like you fanning out from Oakmont into the world, making an impact."

Her words shattered the protective shell that had, to this point, kept me together. I tried to keep my expression exactly the same, but I could feel my lower lip start to quiver and a wall of hot tears build behind my eyes.

"My dear girl, what's the matter?" she said gently.

Dad rose from the table. "Honey?"

And then the tears broke through. Dad rushed around the table and held me.

I struggled to slow down the waves of sobs, gulping for air, as he patted my back. Finally, I could get the words out.

"I'm completely lost."

I started at the beginning—with the night at Festa when Moreno made his offer. Then everything that happened since. I hated telling the details about the car. First the tires, then the brakes. I could see the anguish on Dad's face as the meaning became clear to him. Rage and fear and love coursing through that face, making the muscles twitch and eyes flare. The face that always reassured me that everything would be fine.

Eveline moved her chair next to mine. She reached over and held my hand. Such comfort in her touch.

"For as long as I can remember," I said, "I've wanted to do this work. Now, I'm starting to question everything. Am I able to do this? Do I even want to try?"

"You're not alone in this anymore," Dad said. "We'll figure it out."

We put our jackets on to walk Eveline down to the retreat house where she was staying. Darkness had fallen and we walked beneath a thousand shivering stars, the salt air frigid in our lungs. When we climbed the steps to the porch and reached the front door, Eveline turned to hug Dad, then me.

"Remember the psalm," she whispered in my ear. "The Lord watches over the innocent."

Back at the cottage, Dad lit a fire in the woodstove. I sat curled on one end of the couch, him on the other.

"You should have told me when all this started," he said.

"Didn't want to worry you."

"I worry every day anyway, so just let it all hang out from now on, okay?

I nodded.

"Truth is, I've been keeping something from you too," he said. "The timing is not the greatest. At first, I didn't know what was happening. Then I wanted to wait until I could tell you in person."

My mind raced with horrible possibilities. Was he ill? He took some kind of medicine for his heart. Or some kind of legal trouble?

"Remember when I told you about Eveline leaving the order? How she said she felt unmoored from her calling? I didn't know it then, but weeks later she confided that the reason she left was because she had…these…feelings…" His whole demeanor was like that of a child explaining something difficult. He looked down as he spoke, never meeting my eyes.

Of course. Here I was, a trained observer, and I had missed all the signs.

"Feelings for you," I said.

He finally looked me in the eye. "Yes. Apparently, for many years." He exhaled in relief.

Silence.

"Wow. That's heavy stuff."

He stood up and went over to stoke the fire. "The funny thing was, once she told me, it was like, I don't know, like putting on glasses for the very first time. Everything is so amazingly sharp and clear and beautiful. You can't believe that you've been missing so much."

The full meaning was starting to sink in. This wasn't one-way, was it?

"I love Eveline."

For what seemed like too long, I couldn't speak. Dad standing there by the fire, talking with me as two adults would talk. I thought about all those years he'd spent alone. And how I felt with Eric. And how lovely and warm and good Eveline was. Amid all the frightful, ugly things circling me, this was a victory for the good guys.

I sprang from the couch and buried my head in his chest. He wrapped his arms around me.

"I'm happy for you."

By first light the next morning, Dad had a plan.

He was sitting at the table in the sunroom with his coffee when I got up. The room was snug, with thick jalousie windows all around that stubbornly held back the chill. The dawn had begun to light up the trees, awakening the birds.

"I'm going back with you."

I wasn't sure what he meant.

"Like, to visit for a while?"

120

"No. To stay up there until you solve this thing and we see the dirty bastards hauled off to jail."

I sat down at the table next to him.

"I know you want to protect me, but…"

"No 'buts.' Did you really think I could hear that somebody tried to kill you, and then just smile and wave as you drove back to that all alone? 'Bye honey, be careful!' Nope. Not a chance."

His plan was to rent a larger apartment or house in West Wicklow where all of us could stay for the time being. Eveline, too, if she could get away. Dad would be able to keep up with his caseload by phone and come back to Philly for court appearances when needed.

"They know where you live," Dad said. "This is really the only way."

I had to admit that the idea of having family around calmed some of my worst fears. I had tried to imagine myself returning to work, coming home to that apartment by myself on dark nights. Being on my own in the world didn't seem all that desirable anymore.

But there was still something else holding me back. That older, more elemental fear. *Not everyone is cut out for this work.* Schramm's soul-crushing words coming back once again to haunt me.

"I'm not sure I want to go back."

Once the words left my lips they became real. Impossible to ignore, like smoke signals hanging in the air between us. Dad looked surprised. Disappointed? No, it was closer to the look in his eyes when I would hurt myself as a child. Like he wished he could extract the pain and transfuse it into himself instead.

"I guess you're the only one who can decide that, kiddo." He rose from the table, paused to rub my shoulder, and carried his cup into the kitchen.

"I know we had planned to take a walk on the beach this morning, but I've got a couple of long conference calls I have to do," he called out over the gurgle of the coffee maker. "Why don't you go with Eveline? It may help you clear your head."

Sunset Beach lay west of Cape May, just beyond the lighthouse at the entrance to Delaware Bay. In summer, tourists came by the carload to gape at the ruins of a World War I-era concrete ship, the S.S. Atlantus, victim of an entrepreneur's dubious plan in the 1920s to turn the vessel into a ferry dock. Before construction could begin, she broke free of her moorings in a storm and ran aground one hundred fifty feet from the beach. In the winters, Sunset was our beach for morning walks, sheltered as it was from the rough wind and chop of the Atlantic side. Even there, the relentless sea continued its slow consumption of the ship's skeleton, and each year we would comment that there was a bit less of Atlantus than there had been the year before.

"I haven't seen it in a long time," Eveline said in the car riding over. "Not since I was a child, really."

I'd picked her up in front of the Wedding Cake. She was waiting there on the sidewalk in jeans, an aqua turtleneck and double-breasted Navy pea coat—an image that struck me as surreal. I had never seen her in anything but a skirt. When I was a child in school, the nuns in my world were creatures who seemed to have emerged fully formed in their long black habits, their clacking rosary beads and veils. Yet as I viewed Eveline now I could suddenly see a whole life, the child she was, the teenage girl, gangly and even awkward, perhaps. The young woman my age.

We drove past the salt marshes, lying low and grassy in mirrors of water, a brisk wind setting the sea oats in motion like dancers. Up ahead, the lighthouse rose. The beach lay just beyond.

"Have you spent much time down the shore?" I asked.

"This has always been a magical place to me."

She began to tell me about her life. Her father was a cop, her mother a homemaker who worked part-time in the office of the local church where they lived in Topeka, Kansas. Eveline was their first and only child, and when she was four her father moved the family to Philadelphia for a job on the force. They discovered the ocean ninety miles away and life was never the same.

"We would pack up the car and drive down here every weekend we could. I would wait and wait for that first breath of salt air, hanging out the window, filling my lungs."

Like me, she had attended Catholic schools. Home and school life intertwined with the parish church. I asked when she decided to enter the convent.

"We used to receive a magazine at home every month that chronicled the wonderful work of missionary priests and nuns, building schools and serving the poor in China, Africa, Latin America," she said. "As a teenage girl in the early 1950s, that was stunning to me. Nuns doing meaningful, life-changing work out in

122

the wider world. Women! In hot, muddy, dangerous places. Not being told to dress pretty and smile sweetly."

So in her senior year of high school, when she had to decide what to do with her life, the choice was easy.

"I never thought of it as giving up something," she said. "I knew I could have more freedom to serve God and help other people, to make a difference in the world, by becoming a nun. To me, it was by far the more exciting path."

She looked over at me with a sly smile.

"And I guess it helped that I didn't have a steady boyfriend at that point."

We reached the beach and parked, one of only a handful of cars in the lot on this grey morning.

I sank my hands deep into my jacket pockets against the chill and Eveline did the same. Together we walked toward the water's edge. Seagulls soared in circles above our heads, releasing their urgent cries.

"Atlantus looks much diminished," Eveline said. "In my memory it stood there like a mighty giant."

She was right. What remained of the ship appeared as though it was kneeling on the sea floor, arms of rustled metal in the air, trying to keep its head above water.

We walked together along the shore, the incoming tide chasing our feet. The solitude and the rhythm of our strides created the sensation that we were in a world apart, where I could ask any question, no matter how random or deep.

"How did you decide that leaving was the right thing?"

She stopped and gazed out toward the bay, breathing in deep.

"After much thought and prayer and, I suppose, anguish, I realized it was the only thing I could do."

We continued walking. I pressed to learn more.

"What I'm trying to figure out, for me, is when you have something that you've always believed is your calling, and then something happens that shakes your faith in that, how do you know what to do?"

She squinted as a stray beam of sunlight found its way through the cloud bank that hovered over the sea. "Your calling will always find you. You can't hide from it, even if you try. You see, I left the convent, but not the calling. I knew I could never give up the work I did as a nun. There are people in need everywhere. We just have to see them."

We walked on for a time. Then she stopped and turned to face me.

"Fear is a perfectly rational response for someone in your situation, you know," she said matter-of-factly. "You'd be crazy not to be afraid. You just have to decide how badly you want to keep going."

She stooped down on her haunches to pick up a clear pebble from the sand.

"Do you suppose this could be a Cape May diamond?" she asked, holding it up to the light.

It was part of the strange lore of this place. The beach had a surface of small, smooth pebbles, and mixed among them were quartz crystals that could be polished to a sparkling finish for jewelry. During the high season, the beach was covered with fortune-seekers of all ages, digging through the ordinary tan and grey pebbles, looking for a diamond.

I shrugged. "Who knows? Anything's possible."

She stood up and placed it in my palm, folding her hand over mine and squeezing it lightly.

"Keep it for luck," she said. "A little bit of Cape May to take back to West Wicklow."

I guess she knew I'd made my decision, even before I did.

Chapter Thirteen

By Saturday, Dad had arranged to rent a large furnished house near my apartment. Three bedrooms, one for each of us. I would keep my lease with Francie and be able to stop by to get my mail each day (and any messages from The Postman) on the way to work. On Sunday I drove back, Dad following me in his car with Eveline.

When we reached the house, I realized it was one I had passed and admired in my roamings around West Wicklow. It lay at the end of a long, straight lane that bordered a public golf course at the top of the hill, not far from the more exclusive course that had served as my runaway car ramp. As we drove along, a pair of hardy young golfers in parkas with bags slung on their shoulders trudged up a straw-colored fairway.

The two-story house was sheathed in crisp white clapboards and black shutters, and, importantly for thwarting those with designs to tamper with the Hornet, it had a two-car garage that led directly into the house. Inside, we packed away our belongings. It felt like settling into a hotel for an extended vacation, yet so much more somber. The few things I had with me looked meager in the top drawer of the chest. I would need to bring more from my apartment.

In the kitchen, Eveline sat at the table, making a grocery list to stock up the refrigerator. I looked out the window over the sink. It was a view to the east, across the wintry fairways, beyond the spires and mill towers of the Valley, all the way to a patch of blue bay in the far distance. Ironic. *I may be in semi-hiding, but on the positive side, I have a water view.*

We all got in Dad's car so we could stop at my apartment and then the supermarket. As we pulled into the driveway, Francie looked up from the pile of leaves she was raking in the yard. She let the rake fall and ran over to hug me. I introduced everyone and explained what was happening.

"I'm so relieved! I've been worried sick about you coming back here all alone." She lowered her voice and leaned in. "I've been keeping a close eye on things here. Lonnie came over and we put a padlock on the door while you were gone. Just in case." She reached in her jacket pocket and handed me the key.

She invited us in for hot chocolate.

"You guys go ahead in—I'll join you in a minute," I said to Dad and Eveline. "I want to run upstairs to grab some stuff and make a few quick calls." In truth, I yearned for a few moments to myself. I had traded independence for protection, a good bargain under the circumstances, but one that left me feeling as though I was moving backward in my life.

Inside the apartment, I dialed Eric's number first. I had called him twice from the cottage but even with Dad trying to make himself scarce, it was awkward.

"You're back," he said.

"I am. And I've brought the reinforcements."

"Good, we can use them." A second of silence. Then he said: "When can I see you?"

I'd been fretting for days that maybe what happened the night before I left wasn't the same for him as for me. Now the urgency in those five words extinguished every worry like a gust of wind on a candle flame. We agreed that he'd come to the house for dinner that night.

"I'll bring that rosé you like," he said. And for the first time in my life, I realized I was part of a couple.

I called Ruskin next. Before I left, he had offered to let me stay at his house "until this blows over." I appreciated the gesture but declined. That would have been even more confining than the Dad-and-Eveline option.

"I'm glad to hear you have family with you now," he said on the phone. "We're all very concerned about you."

He paused. "I have to tell you something else. Ned has disappeared."

On Friday afternoon, Ned had failed to show up to put together the Saturday edition of the paper. Ruskin called his apartment and, receiving no answer, walked over to Ned's place and banged on the door. Nothing. Around nine that night, as Ruskin was editing the paper himself, the phone at the M.E.'s desk rang. It was Ned.

"His speech was very slurred," Ruskin told me. "He kept saying not to worry. And that he was sorry."

126

No. Not this. I remembered that night when we'd talked about his success staying sober. What had knocked him off track?

"He seemed so solid," I said to Ruskin. "He was religious about going to the meetings, leaning on his sponsor."

"It's sad. I know he was very distressed that day at the country club."

Of course. I remembered that look in his eyes. Lost, just like me. I needed to fix this.

I called Eric back.

"Change in plans. Can I rent you as a bodyguard for the next couple of hours?"

Hearing about Ned brought back memories of Uncle Rory. When I was little, he was the funny favorite uncle who brought me charming presents and always left an odd odor when he kissed me on the cheek. I was about ten when he quit drinking cold turkey, to everyone's relief. But about three years into his sobriety, he had what he later called "a slip." Like Ned, he just disappeared one day. Later we learned that he'd boarded a bus for Atlantic City and went on a four-day bender. He finally called Dad, who wired him money for a return bus ticket.

Now I was playing a hunch, heading south with Eric in his Jeep. I'd introduced him quickly to Dad and Eveline when he arrived, promising a proper get-to-know dinner later that week. It was only four in the afternoon but winter's impatient dusk was already settling over the roofs of the houses we passed. Lamps glowed in the windows. Darkness fell earlier here than in Philadelphia—another quirk of this place, as if it couldn't wait to welcome the shadows, the melancholy dimming of the light.

"Where exactly is this place Ruskin told you about?"

"Exactly is probably not the right word. He said Ned told him once that he'd spent Memorial Day weekend at a little motel near the ferry terminal in Galilee."

I explained to Eric about Uncle Rory and how he'd said he needed to go to a place where nobody knew him, where he could just disappear.

The night turned wet and mean as we passed Narragansett on Route A1A. A strong wind blew off the Atlantic, changing the falling rain to ice as soon as it hit the windshield. Eric hunched over the wheel, eyes locked on the road ahead. On the front of a waterfront restaurant, a striped summer awning flapped violently. Few cars passed, and, when one did, the beams of the headlights bounced off the slick black asphalt in a blinding display.

"If we manage to find him, do you think you can convince him to come back?"

"I guess I haven't thought that far ahead." I just wanted Ned to know I was okay. That we were fighting this thing together. He was too good a newsman—hell, too good a man, period—to let this swallow him up.

Soon, the long, straight road into Galilee emerged in the mist. I'd driven down here one bright Sunday in August, soaking in the long vistas of salt marsh and glimpses of the blue ocean, cars and bikes passing, kids walking on the shoulder with their floats and beach gear. Now, it looked like a landscape from a frozen planet, the seagrass brown and shuddering, nothing in the distance but blackness.

Finally, up ahead, the lights of the ferry terminal twinkled like a small city.

"I came down here once in the winter to check it out," Eric said. "The ferry to Block Island runs year-round, but this time of year there's only one boat out in the morning and one back in the evening. Still, the commercial fishermen keep working unless they get iced in, and there are some year-rounders, so a few places stay open."

Across from the ferry terminal sat a large seafood restaurant with its lights on and a few cars parked outside, none of them Ned's. We drove up and down the main road and saw just one other business open, a small bar with a neon Miller High Life sign lit. No patrons visible through the window. The few motels along the strip were shuttered for the season.

"Let's take another pass through," I said.

As we traveled back on a side road, I could see a few lights near the back of the seafood restaurant. "Let's try over there."

Eric steered into the parking lot of the restaurant and drove toward the back. He turned at a row of dumpsters and there, on the other side, was a low concrete block structure with a handful of units. A sign on a short pole said: The Ferryboat Inn.

A few cars were parked in front. As we inched past them, I looked for Ned's car. My heart sank as we approached the last vehicle, a large black pickup. But then, hidden on the other side was a beat-up VW Beetle, washed-out aqua paint, the rear bumper covered with stickers. A tattered *McGovern '72*. It was Ned's.

Light shone around the edges of the curtains in the unit directly in front of the car.

"Let me go in alone," I said.

Eric nodded. "I'll be right here."

I knocked, glancing up at the peep hole above my head. I was just about to try again when Ned opened the door.

"What on earth?" he said, looking first at me, then over my shoulder at Eric in the waiting Jeep. He was barefoot, in jeans and a faded red sweatshirt, his face gray and sunken. My eyes darted around the room. No open bottles or glasses. The wastebasket on the floor behind him was overflowing, an empty Southern Comfort bottle planted upside down at the top.

"Don't worry," he said, "I've been sober almost twenty-four hours now. Come on in."

I stepped inside and sat on a straight chair by the window, him on the edge of the bed. The room reeked of cigarette smoke. He reached for a pack on the nightstand and lit one.

"I would ask how you found this needle in a haystack, but then again…" A weak smile crossed his lips.

"Yeah, being a reporter and all…"

"That you are."

"And you're a managing editor."

He hung his head. "Not anymore."

"Don't say that. Come back with us tonight. Ruskin wants you back."

He looked up over the rim of his glasses. "Did he say that?"

"I'm saying it. We can't finish this without you."

I moved over to sit on the bed next to him. "What happened?"

He took a long drag. "Combination of things. My mind racing ahead, thinking that this story of yours was going to be my big redemption. I was back. The Pulitzer-prize-winning editor. Shit." He stuffed the cigarette out in the glass ashtray. He turned to face me.

"Flying a little too close to the sun, right? I got cocky. Skipping meetings. Didn't need them! Too busy. And then the thing with you and the accident. Ha! Bad choice of words. Definitely not an accident. Christ."

"I'm fine."

129

His eyes drilled through me. "You could be dead. And it would've been on my watch."

I stood. Started to pace back and forth. I was not leaving him there.

"Look. I've been having this same argument with myself. Do I want to keep doing this work? Am I strong enough? I hate to tell you this, but I came close to quitting."

His eyes flashed like I had set off an alarm. I sat down again next to him.

"But you know what I realized?" I struggled to find the right words to explain what made me come back. "There aren't any superheroes in our line of work. Just ordinary people like you and me. With all our flaws. We're the only ones standing in the way of people like Moreno and Ducharme and all the other lying bastards out there who grab what they want without worrying about who they hurt. There's nobody but us to call them out. To dig and dig until we drag it all out into the open."

Ned followed us back to West Wicklow. I kept looking over my shoulder to see if he was still there.

As we started out on the road north, Eric reached out to clasp my hand.

"Our first time alone together in a little while," I said.

"You call that a little while?"

"Four days."

"I realized that I didn't like it when you were gone."

"Oh?"

"Nope. Didn't feel right at all." He let my hand go briefly to put on the turn signal, then quickly returned it to its place enveloping mine. I squeezed it.

"I guess I haven't told you, but this is all kind of new for me," I said. "Feeling this way about someone."

He glanced over at me, then back to the road. "Really? Me too."

"That surprises me," I said. "You must have had a lot of girlfriends. At Penn. And all your sailing friends back on Long Island."

"Sure, I dated, but never anybody serious. Not like this."

I liked the way this conversation was going. I studied his profile as he concentrated on the dark road. Then his mouth tightened briefly

130

into a grimace, as if he had suddenly remembered our predicament, almost forgotten these last few minutes in our light banter.

"You can count on me, Meg," he said. "I'm not going to let anything bad happen to you. Ever."

The next morning on my way to the police station I drove past the *Times* parking lot. There sat the Beetle in its normal spot by the back door. Ned was a little shaky that first day back but then seemed to gain strength by the hour. By day two, he was barking questions at us on deadline just like normal.

For me, those first weeks back to work after the break were like starting a new job. A brand-new routine. Dad and Eveline to see me off in the morning. Lining up one of them, or Eric, to ride shotgun with me when I had to cover a night meeting.

The four of us quickly became intertwined. When we rescheduled dinner at the house with Eric, we all talked shop about social justice issues until past midnight. Another outbreak of Ku Klux Klan violence in Mobile that fall. The chilling rise of American neo-Nazis and their attempt to march in Skokie earlier that summer.

"Ever since I read Anne Frank's diary when I was just a kid, I've wondered how everyday German people went along with that horror," I said. "The madness and the inhumanity. I can understand a small cult of evil. Like the Manson family. But an entire country? Mothers and fathers? Teachers, bank tellers, bakers and candlestick makers…"

Around the table, there were no explanations, just sad nods.

"And the worst thing is," Eric said quietly, "if it happened once on that scale, it could happen again. Even here."

Dad raised an eyebrow. "I wonder about that. I like to think that most Americans have an innate common sense and decency. That we are not easily conned. That we wouldn't put up with such a thing."

Eveline reached over to pat his hand. "We can hope that's true, but we have to be vigilant, always," she said. "Remember those famous words: the only thing necessary for the triumph of evil is for good men to do nothing." She glanced over at me with a smile. "And women."

After that night, Eveline started volunteering at the ASJ office, helping plan a lead poisoning outreach effort like the one she worked on in Philly. Dad, although he wasn't licensed to practice in Rhode

Island, spent time coaching the young ASJ pro bono lawyers on civil rights case law and strategy, discussing the possibility of suing the individual mill owners and the town for violating the civil rights of the neighboring residents.

Meanwhile, Eric and I designed our own form of dating. It was still risky and the ethical muddle still made me uneasy. But we'd made love and the world hadn't come to an end. We would be careful, keep a low profile, until the fire story finally was resolved. We arranged to meet accidently in public places where we could have plausible deniability that we were together. Joel and Sara, having already guessed we had feelings for each other, willingly supplied cover when needed.

I'm not sure how I made space inside my brain and heart to fit everything that was consuming me during those December weeks. I was so focused on the investigation and yet so love-drunk with this man that it felt like I was living some intensified version of my life, where everything was in overdrive.

One Friday night after Joel and I finished our late shift at the paper, we picked up Sara and Eric and headed up to a Providence bar called Lupo's, a legendary music venue that could always be counted on to have a good rock band playing well after midnight.

In front of the bar on a deserted stretch of Westminster Street, patrons milled around or sat on the curb, jolted periodically by the thunderous music that spilled out each time the door opened. Inside, the place was dark and packed, vibrating like a giant washing machine with an uneven load.

We got drinks at the bar and inched our way into the thick of the crowd in front of the band, swaying to a driving beat and screaming lead guitar. With music so loud, conversation was limited to nods and gestures. Eric had ordered a Guinness and he pointed at his glass: did I want a taste? I'd never tried it, figuring that it appeared strong and bitter, but now the idea of sharing his beer gave me a warm feeling inside. I took a sip. Smooth and vaguely nutty, not bitter at all. Eric smiled. When we were close together and he smiled like that, it always looked as though he might kiss me, or wanted to. I could feel some of the beer froth clinging to my upper lip, and he reached over to gently smooth it away.

As the band heated up, he looped his arm around my waist and we rocked together to the steady beat, an anonymous party of two.

My "accident" changed the vibe in the newsroom in ways both sad and inspiring. Fewer wisecracks. More serious faces. It had been an attack on all of us, on the work we did. Everyone watched out for one another, offered to team up on stories. Strength in numbers. It felt like lost innocence, but also determination.

One afternoon during the week after the attack, Maddie suggested we meet at Mugsy's to talk.

"My family's pressuring me to quit." Her usually bright eyes looked weary.

"They're frightened for me, and I love them so much and don't want them to worry, but I am not giving up this job, Meg," she said. I had never heard her voice sound so strong.

"So what did you tell them?"

She managed a grim smile.

"I told them that you were a certain kind of reporter. That you investigated serious things. And that I covered things where everybody is happy and smiling. Nobody's going to go to war with a features reporter. I'm like…Switzerland."

"And that seemed to satisfy them?"

"For now."

"But just so we're clear between us," I said, "you know that you have the ability to be that certain kind of reporter, too. If you want to be."

"I know," she said. "Right now, seeing what you're going through, it's not looking all that appealing. But I appreciate the vote of confidence, sister."

I continued working on the mill fire story up in the war room, but I had nearly exhausted all my leads. Meanwhile, the West Wicklow police had hit a dead-end in their investigation of my brake-line cutting incident. Pelletier told me my car turned up no prints or other evidence, and interviews with neighbors surrounding Francie's property produced nothing.

One morning when I stopped to check my mailbox at Francie's, I found a new message from The Postman:

Did you know that the FBI has an office in Providence? Your last story on the inventory lost in the fires may have triggered something there.

Interesting. I'd wondered if that story might have caught the attention of someone outside the reach of whatever corrupt web of influence was operating in West Wicklow. Back in the newsroom, I shared the note with Ned.

"At least from my experience, the FBI will never confirm the existence of an active investigation. All you can do is try to get some sources to confirm that the FBI's on the case," he said.

I thought about this latest note from The Postman. "It sounds like he must have some kind of ties to law enforcement. How else would he know?"

Ned shrugged.

"Maybe. But it's a small town. Gossip oozes like sap through this place."

I needed to find a friendly source. I returned to my desk and found the home number I had for Councilwoman Boucher.

"How are you, Meg?" she said. "I was horrified to hear what happened to you. Just unthinkable. I'm ashamed for our town."

I was flustered by the kind words but glad for the invitation to talk about the fires.

"Mrs. Boucher, I've received some information from a source that the FBI is now looking into the fires, particularly this potential discrepancy in the value of inventory lost. Are you aware of that?"

She was silent for a moment, then spoke in a halting voice.

"Just between us, we've been strictly instructed not to say a word about the FBI coming into this."

I took a breath. "So, the information I've received from my other source is correct, then?"

Silence again.

"Oh what the hell," she said. "Since you've already heard it from somebody else, yes, the FBI is looking into this. Good lord, there's enough secrecy in this town. I'm sick of it."

I didn't want to burn her. Or put her in harm's way. She might not have realized that she was on the record.

"Mrs. Boucher, do you prefer that I quote you as a 'highly placed official in town government,' or use your name?"

"Hell no, I'm no anonymous source! I'm a damned elected councilwoman in this town and I will not hide. Use my name, Meg. Use it, and let's see these slimeballs try to accuse you of making this up!"

As Ned predicted, the FBI office in Providence would not confirm the investigation but we went with a story on the councilwoman's statement in that day's paper. I expected that after that, Ruskin might get another threat from the town solicitor, or that Moreno might spew more insults about the lying press now being in cahoots with his political enemies. But instead, all was quiet. Eerily so.

Later that week, I got a call from Eric at work.

"Hey, I think I might have a lead for you. Remember Marty from that first interview at the mill?"

"Sure. Good guy."

"Yeah, he comes by the office here all the time for the free coffee. This morning, he said he found something over at Hawthorne Mill he wants to show us. Some kind of stash of goods. He was having trouble describing it. You remember, he's a little disconnected at times. He said it would be easier if we stopped over there and he'll show us."

"Probably worth checking out," I said. "You going to play bodyguard again?"

"Of course. I'm going to start charging you at some point, you know."

I loved the easy way we talked. Thinking back to my awkward dates from the past, making conversation then was like trudging across a desert. With Eric, words flowed back and forth as easy and constant as the tides. How far we'd come since that day on the beach.

My mind started to race ahead. For so long, I'd felt like a lone traveler on the earth. Now, I couldn't stop daydreaming of things we would someday do together, places we'd go. I would take him to Cape May. He'd told me about fishing off his sailboat, about how he'd caught a flounder not far from the beach where we'd sat. In West Cape May, we would rent a small skiff and prowl the inlets. I'd teach him how to catch a crab on a slippery green handline. He'd teach me how to fish, and we'd cook our catch on the grill behind the cottage, and after we consumed a bottle of wine with dinner I would fall asleep in his arms.

It was early afternoon when we met at Hawthorne Mill. I passed it every day on the way to the paper, a familiar landmark at the base of the hill. It was the only mill in town constructed of wood instead of stone, clad in a faded indigo blue painted clapboard with distressed white trim. It always reminded me of an abandoned church.

I parked next to Eric's Jeep in the lot. He and Marty got out and we entered through an unlocked back door that Marty knew about.

We walked through the first room inside, a cavernous space illuminated by a shaft of sunlight streaming through the large window at the peak of the structure. No trace of a soul or sound.

"So, you saw something interesting, huh, Marty?" I asked.

He nodded. "Right through here it was." We crossed the threshold into another, smaller space.

Suddenly, behind us came the heavy sound of an industrial metal door rolling, rolling. We all spun around. It slammed shut with a bone-chilling clang.

Marty's eyes went wide.

"Hey, that's not right!" he cried. "The guy's supposed to be here to talk to you."

"Marty, what did you do?" Eric shouted.

Tears streamed down Marty's face.

"A guy gave me some money. He said he just wanted to talk to the lady reporter."

Chapter Fourteen

Marty looked pleadingly at me.

"I know you like to get information. You even wanted to talk to me."

Eric started looking around, frantic.

"No, no, no!" He grabbed a notch in the door and pulled against it with all of his strength. Nothing.

Then, an explosion. The force knocked us all to the ground. Black smoke filled the room as flames flared up from one corner and spread like orange snakes across the wooden floor.

I must have hit my head because everything seemed disjointed. So much smoke. I saw Marty on the ground, not moving.

There was Eric standing over me. So relieved to see him. He grabbed a long piece of lumber from the floor. A two-by-four. But then I got confused and started thinking he looked like a picture I remembered from a storybook. It was about Don Quixote and he had a long, long spear. Eric was jousting with the spear. Jousting at the window behind us. I could see all the windows along the wall and the orange flames flickering in them like candles at Christmas time. I thought about Christmas and Dad. Singing in the choir. *O Holy Night.*

And then I heard a sound, like the keys at the far right end of the piano. No, like glass breaking. Don Quixote broke the glass with his spear. Lifted me onto his shoulders, up to the window sill. Knocking the jagged glass away. *No, you'll cut yourself.* Pushing me up and out. *No, come with me.* I said the words but I don't think they came out.

I fell. A blast of frigid air on my face. Then everything went black.

I woke up in the ambulance, an IV in my arm, machines beeping. The paramedic's face loomed over me.

Where's Eric?

The next thing I remembered was opening my eyes in the hospital room. Eveline sat in the chair next to the bed, a set of crystal blue rosary beads laced through her fingers. In the corner Dad was sitting in a chair, his head tilted back against the wall.

"She's awake!" Eveline said, and Dad sprang to his feet. He leaned over me, brushing back damp curls from my forehead.

I had never seen him cry.

"I'm okay, don't worry," I said, my voice sounding like an old phonograph, my mind sticky like cotton candy. There had been an explosion, I thought, and then some trickles of memory began to flow back and panic shot through me.

"What about Eric?"

Dad looked regretfully over at Eveline and back to me. The tears started to fall again and he started shaking his head slowly.

"No, don't tell me that. No, no." I wanted to stop everything— time, the world turning. Push it all backwards.

Eric was a person alive in this world and now he wasn't? Just like that. Was that what a life amounts to? Something erased so quickly? All those dreams I'd let myself start dreaming were erased, too, with the same swipe.

Dad took my hand, squeezed it.

"He saved you," he said. "The lieutenant told us Eric tried to save the other man, too, but the smoke and flames were too intense."

I had only begun to really know him, and yet I knew that going back for Marty was exactly what he would do.

"Wait," I said, my brain still processing things in random order. "Which lieutenant?"

"The one we saw in the restaurant that night, Pelletier. He stopped in earlier to check on you. Said he wouldn't rest until he brought whoever did this to justice."

Pelletier. I couldn't think about that right now. Just flashes of Eric in that hell. Then him being cold. So cold and all alone.

"He didn't have any family here," I said.

"His parents and brother are driving up to take him home," Eveline said. "The nurse told us."

There would be a funeral. How would I get there? Everything seemed impossible and upside-down.

I realized I had no sense of time. "How long have I been here?"

Dad shook his head. "I've lost track," he said, glancing at his watch. "It's almost midnight. They brought you in at about three this afternoon. They did some tests and gave you something for pain and to help you rest. You've been drifting in and out."

I was having trouble making sense of everything.

"What else did Pelletier say about what happened?"

Eveline patted my hand. "Don't try to remember everything, just take it slow."

"No, I want to understand…" I was so, so tired. But antsy at the same time.

Dad stroked my forehead gently. "Pelletier said you were lucky that the explosion itself was relatively small. It was rigged to ignite the fire in the room where you were. It spread very, very quickly. There was no chance for…" He stopped. I didn't really want to hear more.

Later, a doctor came in and said I had a minor concussion but all of the neurological tests looked good. I had some cuts from the broken glass. My back was badly bruised in the fall, but nothing was broken. I'd be discharged in a few more days if I kept improving. Then continued rest at home through the end of the week. No exertion, no driving, no travel. My brain, especially, needed time to heal.

I started to cry for the first time. Sobs that came from someplace so deep they left me gasping for air. I would be confined to bed while somewhere on Long Island, Eric's family and everyone who loved him would be saying goodbye. He meant everything to me, my today and my tomorrow, and I wouldn't even be on the list of mourners at his damn funeral.

After the doctor left, I convinced Dad and Eveline to return to the house and get some rest. They left the television turned on in the room, tuned to a channel that played old black-and-white movies. Bette Davis with a long cigarette holder and lots of screaming. Everything seemed senseless and I wanted to throw the water glass on my bedside table right through the screen.

I snapped off the light and lay back against the pillows. The only other person I'd ever lost was my mother and I was so young, I only remembered feeling confused at first, wondering where she had gone. It was in the years that came after that I began to grieve for her. In small moments. I would see the mothers of my girlfriends and imagine what she would have looked like in her thirties, then forties. At whatever age I pictured her, she always remained that same beauty, dabbing on perfume at her dressing table as I watched.

On that day Eric kissed me on the beach, I wished I could have run to her afterwards, curled up beside her, told her how full my heart felt, what sublime confusion. Now I wished so many things.

139

That she could have known him. That she knew how much I loved him. That she could hear the sound of my grief piercing the clouds.

I slept, woke and cried. Again and again in cycles through an endless night. Finally, when the pink light of dawn seeped through the cracks between the window blinds, the tears ran dry.

After a while, Pelletier appeared in the doorway.

"Are you up to a visitor?"

I nodded.

"I'm sorry about Eric. He was a good man."

I couldn't say anything. He needed to take my statement and I told him what I could remember. Fragments. I thought surely I would cry when I got to the part where Eric saved me, but no tears came. Wasn't he worth more tears than that?

"We're going to get to the bottom of this thing now, thanks to you—and Eric," he said.

I still wasn't sure where Pelletier fit into this puzzle and I was too mad and weary to dance around it.

"There's a tip you should pass on to the FBI," I said, my voice still labored, croaking. "I understand that in any organization, the bookkeeper is very important."

The color drained from his face. He pulled the chair closer to the bed and sat down.

"How did you know?"

"Lucky guess."

"Nothing on the record. There's still too much work to do."

"Understood. "Why did you help me?"

"Let's just say it became clear to me that this was too big. And there were too many roadblocks. I sized you up as someone who barrels through roadblocks."

A nice compliment, but ill-timed. I wasn't going to be barreling through anything for a while. Still, I wanted to know more. "Is Ducharme the target?"

He looked unsettled to hear Ducharme's name spoken out loud. He glanced around.

"Let the FBI do their job," he said in a low voice. "You've set them on the trail and they'll follow it wherever it leads. But you need to be careful. Lay low."

That afternoon, Joel and Sara came by.

"We wanted to come last night but your Dad said they were limiting visitors," Joel said. His face appeared as though every good and happy thought had been drained out of him. Sara managed a trembling smile.

"Are you in pain? Can I hug you?"

I reached out my arms and she held me for a moment, then Joel wrapped his arms around us both. My tears began to flow again.

They pulled up chairs and sat for a while, one on each side of the bed.

I looked at Joel. "Were you there? At the scene?"

Sara drew in a sharp breath. Joel hung his head.

"I heard the call on the scanner. I was there." He looked up at me. "I don't think I'm able to talk about it, Meg…"

Sara reached over and took my hand. "It's probably best for you, too, not to…"

They were right, of course. I could imagine well enough what Joel had seen. I saw those images every time I closed my eyes.

For the rest of that week, the entire newsroom crew took turns with Dad and Eveline, making sure I always had someone to keep me company. On that Thursday, the day before I was scheduled to be discharged, Maddie brought Aunt Ida with her. In her hands, Ida clutched a small basket with a blue gingham cloth lightly folded inside it.

"I remembered how much you liked the pepperoni bread," she said. "I hoped it might help a little." She set it on my nightstand and patted my hand.

"You're very brave," she said, her lip quivering. "I never understood before. You reporters deserve a lot more respect than you get." She glanced over at Maddie. "I'm proud of Maddie for doing something important with her life."

My tears started to flow again. These days they seemed to always be welled up behind my eyes, ready to begin running in rivers down my cheeks at any moment.

Just then, a nurse poked her head in the door.

"Remember, Meg, you need to get up and walk around the halls, morning and afternoon," she said. "Gotta get your sea legs so you can get out of here tomorrow."

Maddie looked back at me. "How about if we walk with you?"

The nurse smiled. "That's perfect. It's good to have friends to lean on. Just in case."

We walked the route I'd taken the day before. Down the pale green corridor, right at the nursing station, left at the elevator bank. Our feet shuffled along the shiny gray linoleum floors. A nurse rushed past us. Another patient in a hospital gown walked by rolling an IV cart, headed the opposite way.

We reached an intersection and I started to turn left but Maddie touched my arm.

"Want to check this out?" she asked, pointing down the hall to our right. The corridor was carpeted and softly lit with sconces. Large framed landscape photographs hung on the wall. An ocean scene, a meadow filled with wildflowers. Above us, a directional sign said "Chapel" with an arrow pointing the way.

"I never noticed that," I said. "Sure."

Maddie opened the heavy wooden door and we stepped inside a small room with two rows of pews on each side. Light streamed in through a blue and white stained glass window and cast squares of light across the pale blue carpet. We were alone.

We sat together in a pew, Ida on one side of me, Maddie on the other. I had never experienced a place so intensely quiet. I could hear my breathing, feel the blood moving through my veins.

I'd forgotten how to pray. Didn't think I'd earned the right to pray, having fallen away for such a long time. Instead I just stared at the swirling blue of the stained glass, a blue like the sea. I thought of a small sailboat carrying me and Eric off to somewhere happy and safe. To Portugal. A sweet memory, but I couldn't taste the sweetness now.

The tears began to rain down again. Maddie and Ida both reached for one of my hands and held on, rocking with me.

"A church or chapel is the best place to be when you're grieving," Ida said in a low voice. "You can let the tears run down your face and there's no embarrassment in it. No one will think you're odd or crazy. Everyone comes with troubles."

We sat there for a time. There must have been clouds sailing by outside. The squares of light on the carpet faded in and out.

Maddie leaned toward me. "Do you remember the church across from the Festa grounds? Our Lady of Perpetual Help?"

I nodded.

"I go there sometimes on my lunch break on weekdays. If I have something to work through in my mind. It's quiet." She paused. "When you come back to work next week if you need a break, to clear your head, I'll go there with you. Anytime you want."

I patted her hand. These days I was so grateful for each small act of kindness, each gentle word. I started to understand better what to say to a person who's lost someone they love. Just be there. Let them talk. Prop them up. Hold their hand when they cry.

But I knew I could not go back to work this way. So tender and prone to tears. I would have to find a way to grieve for Eric in measured doses. He would want me to keep pushing. Not to wallow, to let myself sink beneath it. I would need to channel every emotion into a determination to get to the bottom of this story. I was sad, but also mad. Anger massed inside me like the tightly wound rubber thread inside a golf ball. Focusing on my anger made me feel stronger. Must nail them and make them pay.

The following Monday morning, I was back at my desk in the newsroom. The staff moved gingerly around me as if I were a fragile piece of china. Joel patted my shoulder on the way to the darkroom. Maddie looked concerned and offered to get lunch for me whenever I was ready so I wouldn't get too tired out. Ned and Ruskin both told me to take it easy my first week back, but I needed to keep moving forward.

I looked through the issues of the paper that I'd missed. Bob had written the stories on the explosion and the deaths of Eric and Marty. From Eric's obituary, I learned the name of the cemetery where they had buried him. I would drive down there next weekend. Snow was in the forecast, but the thought of being there, even on a cold December day, warmed me.

Ned had arranged for Bob to keep covering the police blotter in the mornings for another week to make my re-entry easier. "Let's assign you some lighter stuff for the first few days," he said, handing me a slip of paper with information written on it. "Rosie took this call. Family out in Cheshire has five generations all under one roof right now, visiting for the holidays. You might be able to turn it into a nice little feature. Borrow Maddie's camera and see if you can get a good shot of them lined up from youngest to oldest."

It was the kind of story I covered in my first few days on the job, before my plate filled up with mill fires. Now I felt relief to catch an assignment so simple and sweet. If I could get through this first day without breaking down, I knew it would get easier.

The drive out to the far western reaches of Cheshire helped clear my head. The two-lane road wove its way through farm country, and a light crust of snow covered the rolling fields. Smoke curled from farmhouse chimneys. Chillier out here. I turned up the heat in the Hornet. Every now and again, a bend in the road would bring me into a small village with a few modest houses and businesses clustered closer together, and then another bend would return me to the open road once again.

In one of those hamlets I found the street where the note directed me to turn. I pulled into the gravel driveway of a dilapidated cottage with peeling, white-painted clapboards and a bowed roof. I parked between a rusty pick-up truck and a newer model sedan, walked to the door and knocked.

At first, I heard nothing. Then the muffled voices of two women. "I called them," one said.

The door opened to reveal a tall, sixtyish woman with a strained smile.

"Are you from the *Times*?"

"Yes, someone called. Five generations?"

She had the weary expression of someone resigned to whatever might happen. Nodding, she let me enter.

I stepped immediately into a dim sitting room with an assemblage of some dozen people of all ages: older ones squeezed onto a tattered couch or standing by the heavily curtained window, two children playing Scrabble on the floor, a woman in her twenties in an upright recliner feeding a bottle to an infant. The air in the room felt thick as I drew it in, and above my head, the ceiling tiles looked low enough to brace with my hand.

A woman approached me. She might have been in her forties, with features that suggested she could be the daughter of the woman who opened the door.

"I'm the one who called," she said. Her energetic voice ripped through the silence. She guided me by the elbow. "Let me show you."

Over her shoulder, the older woman met my eyes and locked on.

I was led into the adjacent bedroom, where the light was lower still. In a hospital bed against the wall sat a sallow man in blue pajamas, propped up with pillows. He was thin as a bundle of kindling, his eyes like deep bowls connected by yellowed parchment. I was so startled by his appearance that I almost cried out, but then stifled the sound, leaving my mouth open in the shape of an "O."

"We'd like to get a picture with all five generations around him," the woman said. I could hear her orchestrating the others to come in, positioning them around the bed. The man himself never uttered a word or looked directly at me. On the edge of the gathered group, the older woman bit her lip and looked into my eyes as if determined to transmit her thoughts to me, shaking her head so slowly from side to side that the movement was barely perceptible.

I snapped a photo that I knew would never be published. This was not the time or place for a reporter or a camera. I would ask Joel to make one print and have Rosie send it to the family if anyone called to inquire. But I hoped they had shoeboxes and albums full of photos to remember him, laughing and vigorous in his youth.

On the way back to the paper, I had to pull off the road to gather myself. I parked on a gravel strip and gazed out over a crystal lake, frozen around the edges with a deep blue watery center. No sign of life anywhere. Bare branches against a white sky. I thought of the younger woman, the one who had called. Why on earth would she want a newspaper to document and share such a scene? It defied logic, and yet, perhaps logic became inoperable in such times. Put on a brave face, orchestrate a photo op. Anything to avoid confronting the reality of death, sitting upright before you in blue pajamas.

I had seen a gaunt face like his one other time, but had pushed the memory down so far that it had not surfaced for many years. My mother in a hospital bed like that, set up in the dining room. Day after day. The low murmurs of Dad and the doctor. I learned the word "cancer." The monster that turned her beautiful green eyes into bowls, sunken deep and far away.

Perhaps it was too soon to expect a tearless day. I let gravity pull the tears down, across my cold cheeks, over my lips. A sad kind of saltiness. A red-tailed hawk soared over the lake and then turned toward a lone patch of green in the distance—a sturdy pine on the far shore. I stared at the lake's blue center and willed myself to see Eric's face in sharp focus in the front of my mind, his strong profile, the brown eyes looking out to sea, life coursing through him. Our generation was just beginning. This should not have been his time. I wondered if I would always feel this beaten down.

I got back on the road and stopped at a convenience store to call Maddie. Could she meet me at that church? Just tell me when, she said.

The sign in front of Our Lady of Perpetual Help promised that it was open all day, every day until six o'clock in the evening. *Good to know.* I needed a refuge. I entered through a propped-open door on the side and saw Maddie standing in the back. She embraced me and we sat down together in the last pew.

"Do you want to talk?" she asked in a muted voice. "It's okay. We're the only ones here."

"I don't know. Maybe we could just sit."

She nodded.

We sat for a time. I studied the stained glass windows and the smooth, cool lines of the stone statues. In this place, I could stop trying to steer my mind.

I thought about Eric and my mother, and if they still existed somewhere, in some form. Such comfort flowed from the mere thought of a heaven. Thick, grassy fields and butterflies. In my college days, reincarnation was a hot topic. Was that heaven? The chance to come back?

I had miscalculated how I would navigate this return to my daily life, to my work. I thought that staying busy, staying focused would let me wall off all of the pain into a separate compartment. Apparently that's not how this works. Perhaps this was my path to surviving. Just understanding that the pain will keep breaking through the wall.

Finally, I leaned over to speak to Maddie. "Most of the time, I'm okay," I said. "But then there are times, like today, when sadness is everywhere I turn. I can't escape it."

She put her arm around my shoulder. "All you can do is keep going. And call a friend when it gets bad."

The next morning I sat down at my desk ready to start all over again. One foot in front of the other. Ned had left me a note with information about another story I could work on, something about the Valley's only remaining blacksmith, still operating out in Scituate. Before I could dial the number to set up an interview, the phone rang.

"It's Darlene. I'm so glad you're okay."

Her voice sounded low and shaky.

"I have someone who wants to talk to you. But she's afraid. It's Joan."

We agreed to meet that afternoon at the house. With its wide open spaces all around, it would be difficult for anyone to lurk nearby unnoticed. Dad and Eveline would be there, and I asked Ned to come, too, as both a witness and advisor. I let Darlene know that she and Joan could pull directly into the open garage and I would close it behind them. Nobody would see them walk in.

Even with those precautions, I could barely recognize Joan exiting the car: large sunglasses covering most of her face and her parka hood and a scarf hiding her blond hair. I led them into the dining room where everyone had gathered. Joan's hand trembled slightly as she removed the glasses and unwound the scarf. She looked paler than I remembered and not as perfectly made up. Just a swipe of dark, raisin-colored lipstick that made her look paler still.

She stood in one spot as if turned to stone.

"Here," I said, offering her a chair at the table.

"Please don't think I'm a disloyal person," she said, looking directly into my eyes.

Darlene put her arm around Joan's shoulders.

"Nobody thinks that, honey," she murmured.

Joan glanced around. "Why are all these people here?"

"I just want to listen to whatever it is you want to tell me. And Ned, here, is my editor, so he's here to help me."

I gestured toward Dad and introduced him.

"He's a lawyer in Philadelphia," Darlene said, as if to vouch for him.

Dad interjected gently, "I can't act as a lawyer here in Rhode Island, but I'll help in any way I can."

I introduced Eveline, who was standing by the window.

"I'm the lookout," she said with a grim smile.

Nervous laughter rippled through the room and the tautness in Joan's body relaxed into a slump. She looked at me.

"You were smart to get some people around you. I have nobody."

"You got me," Darlene said, patting her arm. She looked over at us. "Joan's staying with me and Petey for a little while."

I reached for my notebook and pen. "I want you to know that I will never use your name or tell your name to anyone, unless you give me your permission. And depending on what you tell me, we'll try to help you figure out what to do next."

Joan nodded.

Over the next three hours she told me her story. Eveline made tea and put some cookies on a plate in the middle of the table. Ned moved to the corner of the room and smoked three cigarettes in a row. Dad listened and paced.

I kept writing and filled up one notebook and half of another with her words. Along the way I asked some questions to probe or clarify. But mostly Joan just talked.

Chapter Fifteen

There's a reason I said that to you, about not being a disloyal person. I feel bad about coming to you because Mr. Ducharme has done a lot for me. He gave me my first job. All I had was a secretarial school diploma, but he was willing to give me a lot of responsibility. I liked learning things. Handling important work, and him depending on me. But I realized over the last couple of weeks that you can't stay loyal to someone once you know they're not the person you thought they were.

My mother tried to warn me, a couple years ago, when I first told her he was training me to help him with the books. "Something doesn't add up about this," she said. "Why doesn't he hire an actual bookkeeper?" We had a falling out over that. I thought she was trying to hold me back, like she always did when I was in school. Remember, Darlene? She never believed in me. Never. But Mr. Ducharme did.

Of course, he's always been sort of a mystery man. In high school, that's what we all thought. Someone would see him walking in town, or stopped at a red light in that big shiny Caddy. And the next day at the lunch table we'd talk about him. The richest man in West Wicklow. We'd make up fantasies about one of us marrying him, like Cinderella. So when I heard through the guidance counselor at school that he was looking for a secretary and she had recommended me, I couldn't believe my luck.

He's been a good boss. He wants things the way he wants them, but he's nice about it, you know? One of the first things he did was give me what he called a wardrobe allowance. Every month, there would be some extra in my check. He said it was important to create the right impression for people coming into the office to do business.

There are some people who come in a lot. Mr. Moreno, I've gotten to know him pretty well. They became partners a few years ago in the car wash business. He comes in for meetings regularly. And other people who work for the town. I have no idea if any of this means anything, or fits together, but I'm just telling you. One of the people who started to come in for meetings over the last year was one of the battalion chiefs in the fire department. Chief Nunes.

Mr. Ducharme's businesses are very complex. It took me a while to understand how everything works. There is a large management company, XL Strategies, that oversees most of the mills in town and more all around New England. Each mill is set up as a separate business but Mr. Ducharme is the main investor in each one. I handle the books for XL. Then there's Luxury Holdings, which buys and sells all kinds of high-end, designer clothing and accessories all over the East Coast. Beautiful things. That's a really big operation and Mr. Ducharme has an accountant in New York who handles all that, so I don't have to worry about it. And then there's the car wash business, which Mr. Ducharme said was good for him to have in his portfolio because it's mostly cash transactions at a steady, predictable volume, and that helps with cash flow for his business overall. Somebody at Mr. Moreno's business handles the financials for that. There are dozens of other businesses, too—real estate developments and rental properties—but XL, Luxury and the car wash are the ones that I started to have some concerns about over the last few weeks.

When I read the story you did right before Thanksgiving, the one where you interviewed the firemen about what they remembered seeing in the mill fires, it really unsettled me. I remember entering insurance settlement payments on the XL books as income as we began to receive them for the fires that happened earlier in the year. But they were just numbers to me. I didn't know specifically what was in the claims. But here's the thing: those designer goods would never have been stored in the mills. We have warehouses—I mean Mr. Ducharme has warehouses—that store all of that inventory and distribute it to the retailers.

I was going to ask Mr. Ducharme about it but that next morning he was in his office with the door closed, on the phone, until I had to leave at noon. Then, over the holiday, I saw the story about what happened to you with your brake line being cut. My God. I was so glad you weren't hurt. I remembered talking to you in the office that time. You wanted to interview him about the fires, remember? I really wasn't sure then if you might have figured out that he had a financial stake in those mills. Nobody knows about that. Mr. Ducharme says it's proprietary information and I'm not to disclose it to anyone. But I admired you for coming in there and trying to get an interview. You were just doing your job. I'd never seen him as furious as he was that day. He slammed the door, which never happens. He's always very controlled.

Once I saw in the paper what happened to your car, I started to feel very uneasy about everything. I was having trouble sleeping. Over that weekend, I knew Mr. Ducharme was traveling, so I went into the office. Part of me felt like I was doing something wrong to be digging through files, but I had to figure this out or go crazy.

I brought the copy of the newspaper with me, the one that had the whole list of all the inventory claimed as lost in the fires. I knew where Mr. Ducharme kept his copies of the Luxury financial reports in his office. I dragged out the books and went over them line by line. It took hours. I was shaking. The description of every one of the lots on the claims list matched a description of goods sold and recorded as revenue on Luxury's books this year.

It hit me. What that meant. He was getting money for the same goods twice. Once as a bogus fire damage claim and then again as actual sales. The same goods! It was a strange feeling. Realizing that someone I worked with for three years, someone I looked up to, was possibly involved in something…criminal. That seems unthinkable, to associate that word with Mr. Ducharme. Why would he do those things? He was already rich. And we're not talking just shady business dealings. What do they call that, "white collar crime?" No, these were crimes that actually hurt people. Maybe killed people, even.

As the days went by, this was all weighing on my mind. And I started to get more and more scared. For my safety. Why did he have me do the books for XL? Maybe he was going to blame it all on me somehow?

And what if it's not just Mr. Ducharme involved? I've thought a lot about the car wash business. That was a very odd thing for him to invest in, even with his explanation about cash flow. The whole extent of Mr. Ducharme's involvement in that business is that Mr. Moreno comes to the office at the end of each month, like clockwork. He always carries a briefcase.

One time, Mr. Ducharme had to step out quickly just after Mr. Moreno had left. Then someone called and I had to go into his office to check the calendar on this desk. His bottom drawer was slightly ajar. I could see there was a big manila envelope stuffed in there like it didn't belong. It looked fat, bulging, like when you try to fit too many things inside, you know? It was odd.

I'm just telling you things that jumped out at me. I don't know what makes sense anymore.

I thought about quitting. Just disappearing, actually. Moving to Boston, getting a secretarial job. I have a little of my wardrobe money saved.

But then those awful things happened. The explosion. That nice young guy who died, and the other man. It's like every day it just gets worse and I feel like I'm in a room where the walls keep closing in on me. I even thought about going to the local cops, but God, the council president might be in on this for all I know, so maybe the cops are in on it, too.

When I read that the FBI was looking into it I knew I needed to do something. They might think I'm part of this. They could send me to prison. If someone doesn't kill me first.

I'm sorry to be crying this way. I was determined to get the whole story out without crying.

You're the only person I can trust to help me.

Chapter Sixteen

As Joan spoke, I forced myself to concentrate and take accurate notes, but in a separate compartment my emotions raced ahead. Queasiness mixed with euphoria as I began to see the shape of what I'd been poking at for months. A deep, growling fear for her safety (and mine). And a complete lack of certainty about what to do next. This was a blockbuster story, but definitely not one we could publish without risk of libel, putting Joan in harm's way and interfering with an FBI investigation.

When she finished, I turned to Dad first.

"What do we need to do to make sure Joan is safe?"

He had an old law school friend who specialized in white collar crime in Boston. He went into the next room to try to reach him, and Eveline took Joan and Darlene into the living room to wait.

Ned looked at me and shook his head.

"This is a tricky one," he said. "I had something similar happen with the slumlord investigation. I got some really hot information from a source about a murder committed by one of the building owners. Obviously, you've got to do what's right. So I encouraged the source to go to a cop friend of mine. Then he tipped me off just before they were about to make the arrest."

"So you think I should call the FBI?" I asked.

He paused to light another cigarette. "Let's see what the game plan is with the lawyer. Ideally he would reach out first and set up a time to bring Joan in. But then let's have you also call the FBI contact you spoke to last time. Let him know that you encouraged a confidential source to reach out to them. You'll get some credit for that and hopefully they'll give you a little advance notice when all this is about to go down."

Soon it was all arranged. The next morning, Dad and Eveline would drive Joan to Boston, where she would meet with Dad's attorney friend and visit the FBI field office to tell what she knew. The agent in charge promised to take measures to protect her.

Once Joan had left with Darlene, I waited until late in the afternoon and then called the special agent in the Providence office I'd talked to weeks earlier, Jack Morton. He remembered me, and his tone was different this time. Gone was the buttoned-up, automatic "no comment" that slammed the door on further discussion.

"I'm aware of what you're referring to." He paused. "You did a good thing."

"What happens next?"

"You tell me. You gonna publish anything?"

"Not yet. Not until there's something solid. But I've been working this story for a while and…"

"Don't worry. I know exactly how long. Consider me one of your most faithful readers."

I was taken aback. I always thought FBI agents were supposed to be humorless.

"Look," he said, "you've been a solid citizen. Let's keep in touch. Give me your office number and one where I can reach you after-hours. Just in case anything were to break that you might be interested in."

That night, exhausted and starving from the long afternoon's drama, we all went to dinner together—Dad, Eveline, Ned and I—at the Chinese place on Main. It was one of several restaurants in West Wicklow that I usually tried to avoid. Very early on I realized that in those particular eateries I would always run into some town official or other source I knew. In my first weeks on the job, I reveled in the experience of being "someone" in town, hardly a celebrity, but a small-scale version of that, a person who knew important people and was known by them. The wave and smile on the way to the restroom. The pat on the shoulder. The introduction to so-and-so's wife and kids.

After a time, though, it became stifling. As my mill fire stories began to pile up, I got fewer smiles. Sometimes a surly look from an off-duty fireman or cop. The cursory nod and frown as someone passed my table. Except for Estrella's, which I continued to frequent to keep in touch with Darlene, I found other hangouts in Cheshire or a few miles away in Wicklow where I could eat in peace.

But tonight was different. I was different. Since the explosion. I had a baseline of anger that was never there before, always on now, like the blue pilot light in the gas oven. I was a boxer with gloves raised, ready to punch. *Let's go out among the West Wicklowites who hate my guts. They have no way of knowing the freight train that is about to hit them.*

As we walked down Main Street, a light snow began to fall, coating the tops of the garish illuminated holiday decorations attached to each light post. A large, maniacal Santa face looked down upon us as we passed, and at the next post loomed a bat-like shape that must have been an attempt at an angel. Perhaps it was my own dark mood coloring everything.

Inside, the Golden Dragon was packed, but we found a large, round booth open in the corner. The place was a cacophony for eyes and ears, awash in fluorescent light and cackling conversation that bounced off every Formica surface. Ned and I recognized a few faces among the patrons. The Town Planner and his wife sat in a booth near the front. The head of the Chamber of Commerce was there with a developer I'd interviewed once.

As I looked around at all of the faces, Joan's story rang in my ears. There were people in this town who were not what they appeared to be. I thought about the manila envelope in the drawer. There was no way of knowing how far the infection had spread. Every face, every laugh was suspect. I was reminded of an old science fiction movie in which the aliens were living among us, passing as human. Trust no one.

Ned leaned in.

"So folks," he said with a wry smile, "since we're obviously limited in the subject matter we can talk about, how's everybody's Christmas shopping going?"

On the following Saturday morning, I perched in the tiny backseat of Joel and Sara's Maverick, staring out the ice-crusted window at the cars lumbering by on I-95 South.

"When does the ferry leave?" Joel asked.

Sara squinted at the small type on the schedule unfolded on her lap.

"Eight-thirty. We're in good shape to make it." She looked back at me and smiled in that comforting way she had.

They had picked me up at seven so we could drive to New London, Connecticut, board a car ferry to Orient Point on the tip of Long Island's North Fork, then take a second ferry to Shelter Island, where Eric was. We'd make the return trip tonight.

155

That first day I returned to the newsroom after the hospital, I'd mentioned to Joel that I planned to drive down to the cemetery. He was quick to suggest we all go together.

"You don't always have to go it alone, you know," he said gently. I knew it wasn't meant as a criticism. He was right. I tended to look at things with tunnel vision. All I could see was the gaping hole in my world where Eric used to be. I sometimes forgot that others had lost him, too. I was only focused—hell-bent is a better word—on getting to the spot where he was now. I knew it wouldn't change anything. I just had to get there.

I had another mission, too. While I was still in the hospital I'd gotten in touch with Eric's parents through the funeral director. It was a short, strained phone call with his mother, Jane. *I was a friend of Eric's.* What an incredibly insufficient description. *I hoped I could stop by to meet you, to talk to you about him.* Yes, she said, they wanted to speak to me, too. They had questions.

On the ferry trip across Long Island Sound, we left the shelter of the warm cabin to go out on deck for the last few minutes as the boat neared Orient Point. The deck was slippery under our feet and the three of us clung to one another and the frozen handrail. A merciless wind lashed our faces, mixing salt spray with our tears. These were the waters where Eric grew up sailing. I imagined him standing beside me, his shaggy hair flying in all directions. He was pointing out landmarks, telling stories of harrowing voyages. For the first time since I learned he was gone, I was certain that he wasn't.

The second, smaller ferry deposited us on a grey Shelter Island encrusted with a thin and patchy coating of snow. As we drove, the weak sun cast a strobe effect through the towering stands of pine trees, and the stony blue water of the Sound hid itself and then reemerged at every bend in the road.

Finally, the entrance appeared up ahead. We drove through the gate and followed the directions the funeral home had given me. Left at Row 3. Right at Section B. Down the lane to the end, on the left, under the tree.

I spotted the headstone from the car, all alone on its large plot, the first of his family. After all those days of holding it together, everything blew apart. This was real. Unchangeable. Sara reached back and squeezed my hand.

"Are you okay to get out?"

I nodded. We all walked over together, Joel holding me up on one side, Sara clutching my arm on the other.

We stood in front of the stone, and once we were there, once I saw his name, everything raging inside me went quiet and I felt again his presence. His warm way. His courage. I didn't need to cry. He was still protecting me.

The road to 432 Windjammer Way was a narrow lane made of crushed seashells that crackled under our tires. By the time we arrived it was early afternoon and the sun lit up the stately, shingle-style house at the edge of the Sound. Just beyond it, a long pier extended into the blue. Docks were stacked neatly on the lawn for winter. Closer to the house, a small boat covered with a blue plastic tarp rested on a wooden rack, its mast protruding from both ends. Eric's boat.

The woman who answered the door was tall and trim, in tailored slacks and a pale gray cashmere sweater set. Her hair fell in loose waves in the style of Jackie Onassis, and she wore the light makeup of a well-groomed woman of means—eyeliner, a touch of pale foundation and burgundy lipstick. Her eyes were the only part of her that betrayed a woman in mourning: puffy lids, dark circles and a piercing stare that made me think of two-way glass, cloaking what was on the other side.

With barely a word, she led us through an imposing atrium, past a round, gold-edged table bearing the largest vase I had ever seen, and the tallest gladiolas. Their scent intruded on every breath, a jarring sweetness in the desolation of December. We followed her into the living room and took seats on a long couch while she sat opposite us on a chair upholstered in robin's egg blue.

"My husband was called away." Her voice was colorless.

I conveyed our sympathies, thanked her for seeing us.

I began. "I worked with Eric on…"

"I know very well who you are," she interrupted without raising her voice in the slightest. "My son was in love with you. It was fairly obvious."

I flushed and could feel tears rising. Joel reached over and put his arm around my shoulder.

Her eyes flared.

"Who are you to cry? You knew him for mere days!" She leaned forward, palms pressing into her thighs. "He was...my...child."

The tears rolled down my cheeks despite her disapproval.

"I loved your son..."

"That's not love," she snapped. "That's ambition. I know all about people like you. Journalists. With your supposed high-minded ideals. Like you've been appointed to snoop into other people's affairs. My Eric was so taken in by you. He believed that you were trying to help people."

She paused, tipping her chin down to glare at me.

"You dragged my son into this to sell newspapers. Not even a very good newspaper at that!" She sniffed. "A little rag!" She suddenly rose from the chair and stalked over to a chest by the wall. She threw open the lid and pulled out a stack of newspapers. Back issues of the *Times*.

"I kept telling him this was reckless, what you were 'investigating.' I begged him to stay away from you." She was standing over me now.

"I don't want this garbage in my home!" she said, thrusting the papers in my arms.

"I'm...so sorry..." All of us rose at once. I searched for some words that would set this right.

But now her controlled rage exploded.

"You got my son killed!"

We walked to the door, her behind us.

"Get out! Get out!"

Outside, in the frigid air, I could still hear her shouting.

On the ride home, I sat in the back with my knees pulled up to my chest, arms wrapped around. I imagined making myself smaller and smaller, a tight ball that could be ejected out into space and disappear in the cold black sky.

Joel's sad eyes studied me in the rear-view.

"She was crazy with grief, you know."

Sara turned in her seat to look back at me.

"He's right. The things she said..." Her voice cracked. "This was not your fault."

I knew that. Eric's mother didn't know me. She seemed to not really know her son very well, either. I felt sadder for him, and understood better why he'd set off on his own.

Her sweeping dismissal of the whole profession of journalism was the thing that still stuck in my craw. That line about "you're only in this to sell newspapers!" Wish I had a quarter for every time I heard that one.

If people only knew the truth of it. We didn't give a rat's ass about selling newspapers for Ruskin or any other publisher. That's not what drives me, or any reporter. I wished she understood that Eric hadn't died for something as trivial as that.

Chapter Seventeen

During those late December days, while so many dark and furtive things were happening, the daily news of West Wicklow and the rest of the world played on. Maddie covered the arrival of Santa Claus at the Wicklow Mall, and John was immersed in a three-part series on the impact of a property tax hike in Cheshire. In the "Around the U.S." column, the White House prepared for President Carter's trip to Tehran later that month to visit the Shah.

I waited for the FBI to drop the next shoe. Dad learned from Joan's lawyer that she was safe in an undisclosed location. They had instructed her to call Ducharme and say her mother was having a health crisis and that she would need to take an immediate leave of absence.

I continued my daily routine of checking the police blotter in the mornings. Teddy had gone into a neutral state—not as openly hostile as when I first started digging seriously into the records, yet not cordial or matter-of-fact, certainly not friendly. He barely reacted to my comings and goings at all, as if I were not really there, or perhaps, as if he assumed I would not be there forever, like an odd ache that one dismisses with the belief that it will eventually disappear.

When I dropped by the Detective Division each morning, Pelletier did a masterful job of acting like we never had the conversation in the hospital room. For a moment, I wondered if I had dreamt it.

Pelletier's loyalties in all of this continued to trouble me. I had briefly considered—then quickly dismissed—the idea of enlisting him for advice when Joan came to me. It seemed like too great a risk. He was clearly trying to help me, but I worried there might be some agenda or a larger game being played.

Each night, as I tried to fall asleep, I thought about all of the facts Joan had revealed. One question she asked kept buzzing in my mind, like the fly that passes close to your ear in the darkness. Ducharme was already rich. Why would he do this? The capacity for evil in human beings was an old story, filling the news each day in every town, in every country. Yet, until now, I had not seen it up close, not felt its breath on my neck.

As a journalist, I'd been trained always to seek out the person on the "other side" of the story. Give them the opportunity to comment or set the record straight. I struggled with what that might mean in this case. An image flashed through my mind: sitting across a table from Ducharme in a cold, grey room, taking notes as he explained that this was all preposterous fiction.

The ringing phone woke me from an unsettled sleep. It was Jack Morton.

"Two locations. His office and the car wash. One hour."

The clock read four in the morning. I called Ned, then Joel. Ned lined up Bob to camp out at the car wash; Joel and I would head to the building that housed Ducharme's office.

Dad emerged, sleepy-eyed, from his bedroom as I sprinted out the door.

"It's happening."

We waited in our cars, parked on Main a few doors down from the office building. It was still dark and the deserted street was silent except for the faint clack of a stop light switching from green to red.

Just before five, two black sedans and two state police cruisers rolled up. Out poured a half dozen men in FBI jackets and four uniformed troopers. We got out and Joel started snapping photos. One of the FBI men looked over and gave me a quick head nod. *Must be Morton.* He was tall with a squared-off build like a refrigerator, early thirties, close-cut black hair. He strode over to us.

"You'll have to stay out here on the sidewalk. When we come out I can give you a statement."

A custodian appeared at the door with a big ring of keys and the troopers and FBI agents streamed inside. Over the next two hours, I watched and Joel shot as teams carried out boxes of files, several metal strongboxes and what looked like a small safe with a combination lock.

Morton walked over to me as they appeared to be wrapping things up.

"The FBI field office in Boston assisted by Rhode Island State Police early this morning executed search warrants at the office of RD Holdings at this location, and at Blue Wave Car Wash at 1654

Salem Highway. Both raids are part of an ongoing investigation. The FBI will have no further comment at this time."

I stared at him. *Was that it?*

"Have you made any arrests?"

"No."

"Is this investigation related to the series of mill fires in West Wicklow?"

He cocked his head to one side.

"Off the record?"

"Off the record doesn't do me any good. How about attributed to a 'source close to the investigation?'"

He nodded. "Yes, it's related."

"Are Roland Ducharme and Thomas Moreno targets of your investigation?"

"Look, here's what you can use. Both of those individuals are persons of interest in our investigation."

I wrote furiously to capture his words as carefully as he had spoken them.

Suddenly I realized the significance of actually using those names in my story, in a newspaper that would roll off the press just after noon.

"Let me ask you this—off the record," I said to him. "Aren't you afraid that they'll skip town, or worse? What if they come after the people who are trying to expose them?"

His face creased into a half-smile. "Don't worry, Meg. Off the record, there's not a move either of them can make that we're not aware of. This wasn't kids setting fires for kicks, or even garden-variety insurance fraud. These are homicides."

He paused. "As you well know."

Morton turned to walk to his car, then spun around again.

"Oh, and another thing. The next time I call, you're going to have to send a different reporter."

"What? Why?" This was my story.

"You're a victim. I can't have you there when this next part goes down."

That word was like a gut punch. I knew what he meant, technically, but that wasn't me. I wasn't about to let anyone turn me from a reporter into a victim.

That night, Dad and Eveline sat in front of the television half-watching an episode of *The Love Boat* while eyeing me nervously. I paced, listening for the phone. That day's paper lay open on the coffee table. The names of Ducharme and Moreno screaming in forty-eight-point boldface. Once the paper hit the street, the rest of that afternoon was bedlam in the newsroom. Manuel Perreira, Ducharme's lawyer, called Ruskin and threatened to sue for libel. Moreno called Bob directly and yelled a two-sentence statement professing innocence, decrying "illegal and false leaks by law enforcement" and demanding a retraction.

Just after nine, Morton called.

"West Wicklow Country Club. Half-hour."

I parked on the side of the road and watched as Bob and Joel drove through the entrance gates to the club. I could see tiny white twinkling lights on the spruce trees lining the driveway, and, in the distance, the amber glow of the clubhouse. I rolled down my window. Faint sounds of a band playing a swing version of *I Saw Mommy Kissing Santa Claus*. Later, I would press Bob for every detail, and pour over every print Joel made. The stricken looks of two women in the lobby as the invading entourage moved in. The swirl of tuxedos and long dresses, chandelier light and crystal glassware. The way Morton and his team parted the crowd, which grew gradually quieter the deeper they advanced. Low, urgent murmurs. *What's happening? Who? My God!* Ducharme's well-coiffed head turning toward them. On his face an expression of cool and composed defiance, as if he knew this entire episode were a horrible mistake that he would be laughing about with his clubmates over lunch tomorrow.

"Roland Ducharme, you are under arrest for the murders of Eric Fields and Marty Conway, the attempted murder of Meg Sullivan, conspiracy, 14 counts of arson, 1 count of felony murder in the death of Conrad Baines, bribery and money laundering."

I saw headlights coming down the driveway. As the line of cars sped past me I caught a glimpse of Ducharme in the back seat of a state police cruiser, his chin up, staring off into the black night.

Ducharme wasn't the only one taken into custody that night. Moreno was arrested while dining at Giorgio's, another one of those restaurants in town that I avoided. The FBI team swarmed into the fire station and hauled off Nunes and his four-member crew.

It was close to midnight. Bob, Joel and I camped out in the detectives' conference room at police headquarters. We obtained copies of the arrest affadavits detailing the charges and poured through them under the harsh white light of the fluorescent bulbs overhead. Just outside, the hall was packed with cops, lawyers, FBI men moving in all directions. Through the open door, I could see Pelletier talking with Morton. Friendly tones. Morton gave him a slap on the back, then stopped in to talk to us.

As he outlined it, the conspiracy was bigger and more complex than even I had imagined. Ducharme had assembled all of the necessary pieces. A town council president powerful enough to open doors and make sure investigations didn't go too far. A battalion chief who knew how to set a fire and rig an explosion. A loyal crew of firemen to make sure no evidence of the point of ignition would be left at each scene. And money, tens of thousands of dollars in car wash money, efficiently purified on the books and doled out from manila envelopes to keep all of the parties in line.

I asked Morton about an item in the affidavit that caught my eye. It said an "unnamed member of local law enforcement" had assisted the investigation by posing as a willing participant, accepting the bribe money and providing details to the FBI about conversations with the perpetrators. I asked about the identity of the informant, knowing full well who it was.

Morton just smiled.

"Some details we have to save for trial."

When I finally got home just before two, Dad and Eveline were still up, playing double solitaire at the kitchen table. He rushed toward me.

"Did they get him?"

"They got him. They got them all."

He wrapped his arms around me, relief spreading across his ruddy face into a blissful smile. We rocked back and forth and Eveline came over to join the goofy three-way slow dance.

"*You* got them, Meg," he whispered.

It was starting to sink in. The excavation work was done. All out in the open now. They would pay for what they'd done to Eric, to Marty and Connie, and to all those families driven out of their apartments in the middle of the night. But then a strange new feeling flowed in. The next part was all in someone else's hands now. I wasn't a cop, a G-man or a judge. No more scribblings to make on the war room wall. It almost felt like I'd lost my job.

Ned was already at his desk when I walked into the newsroom a little before six the next morning.

"Strolling in late, eh, Sullivan?" He peered up at me over the tops of his wire-rims and grinned. "Now that you're done saving the world."

I plopped down in the chair next to his desk. I had kept him updated by phone as events played out the night before. There would be a lot to cover this morning. The FBI had scheduled a press conference at 11 at police headquarters and other reporters would be starting to put the story together. The Wicklow news radio station, the daily newspaper and television stations from Providence, the wire services. But the *Times* would be the only one with photos and an on-the-scene report of Ducharme's arrest.

"So," Ned said, "have the post-investigation blues started to hit you yet?"

I was dumbfounded. Was he reading my mind now?

"How did you know?"

He chuckled. "I lived it, remember? How do you think I ended up editing a paper in beautiful West Wicklow?"

Right. He had lived it. Barely lived through it.

He studied me closely.

"Just remember that you have a life beyond this one story. You'll move on to something else."

I nodded.

"But first, there's today's paper to put out," he said. "So, Bob will write the arrest story."

"I was thinking I could start working on an in-depth piece on Ducharme. Track down people who have known him over the years, really try to figure out what makes him tick."

Ned winced. His expression was the one you see just before someone tells you unexpected bad news.

"Meg, somebody should do that profile but it can't be you. Just like you couldn't cover the arrest because you're a victim in this story, I'm sorry but you can't write any of the follow-up stuff either. Not a

166

profile feature, not the press conference, not the pre-trial hearings or the trial."

That part of this entire journey hadn't hit me yet. But he was right, obviously. What reader could trust me to write objectively about people who'd tried to kill me?

"And, it actually gets a little worse," he continued. "It's almost a certainty that other reporters are going to want to interview you about what happened. We need to talk about how to handle that."

The idea of being on the other end of a reporter's interview felt foreign and wrong, like someone suggesting they replace my right arm with one of those long plastic backscratchers.

Later that morning, I saw Ruskin and Ned talking. It seemed like a difference of opinion. Ruskin caught my eye and beckoned for me to come over.

"Meg, I understand that Ned thinks we need to keep you on the sidelines now but frankly, I think we're carrying this objectivity thing a little too far. We can't just pretend that you're not part of this story. I think you should be writing a first-person account—that we'll clearly label as opinion, not news. We'll run it on the front page alongside the story on the arrests. This thing can put us on the map. We can't miss this opportunity."

"Clive," Ned interjected, "I just worry about doing something that would hurt the case and hurt the paper's reputation. They could say we're biased. That this whole thing was a witch hunt. Hell, Moreno's been accusing us of that already, for months."

Suddenly I had a brainstorm.

"You know what might be better than me writing something? How about a front-page editorial?" My eyes were trained on Ruskin. "Something really thoughtful, inspiring even. About the importance of a free press. And how, naturally, we have to let the justice system run its course. Innocent until proven guilty and all that. But that we played the role in this situation that we were supposed to play. The role nobody else can play."

The moment I started talking Ruskin's eyes began to dance.

"A real think piece," he said. "Yes, I like that. Great idea, Meg."

He scurried off to his typewriter in the corner to begin writing. Later, mixed in with the usual chatter and hum of the newsroom, we could hear snippets of phrasing and murmurs of delight with his own words.

"The *indispensable* role of a free press. Yes, that's it!"

167

Just as Ned had predicted, shortly after the press conference, requests for interviews started coming in from other media. Not just Rhode Island reporters but national too. The reporter from *People* was particularly persistent. "You risked your life to bring a corrupt criminal ring to justice," she said. "It's an inspiring story."

I didn't want to be the focus of the story, inspiring or otherwise. I told all of them the same thing: That I couldn't make any comment on a pending criminal case. What I didn't say was that everything of significance that I knew had already been reported either in my stories on the case or Bob's. I understood what they wanted. I would have wanted the same information if I were covering the story. How did it feel to be in fear for my life for months? What was it like inside that mill when the explosion happened? What went through my mind when I learned that the arrests had been made?

I was not ready to talk about any of those things. Not ready to relive those moments, not ready, even, to start letting that tightly wound ball of anger inside unravel. If anyone was going to write about what happened to me, it was going to be me. But not for a long while.

After the paper announcing the arrests hit the streets at noon, the newsroom staff gathered at the Rock to celebrate. The combination of sleep deprivation and a wave of professional euphoria had left us punchy, even before introducing alcohol into the mix. For the first time, Ned came along, drinking non-alcoholic beer while acting as loopy as the rest of us. The traditional stuffies were ordered all around. The more hot sauce we used, the more beer we drank.

By round three, John, in the spirit of black humor beloved in the newsroom, asked the bartender to play the Talking Heads' *Psycho Killer,* and as the crazed lyrics started to pound through the bar, we all spontaneously got up to dance, undeterred by the lack of a dance floor or the annoyed stares of the handful of other patrons. We held imaginary mikes to our mouths and shouted along. *Fa-fa-fa-fa-fa-fa-fa....*

When the song finished, Bob grabbed a stuffie and held it solemnly in the air.

"To Meg Sullivan, who never gave up!"

"To Meg!" they shouted, raising stuffies in unison.

Ned held his faux beer aloft.

168

"To all the lying, scheming, corrupt bastards in West Wicklow. May they rot in hell."

Chapter Eighteen

There were still days when I woke up and thought about calling Eric. Or heard something funny and wanted to tell him. Then reality took hold again and the pain flowed back in like lava, searing me deep inside. But it was worth it. A split second of him alive in my world.

Christmas came and went. I was relieved for the holidays to be over, for a return to normal times when not being merry was acceptable again. Dad and Eveline made plans to head back home. Time for me to restart my old life in the apartment over Francie's garage. An altered version of my old life.

"I'll still worry about you," Dad said as he loaded their gear into his car. "Just slightly less."

Eveline hugged me close.

She whispered in my ear. "Don't feel like you can't afford to be sad. Be sad for as long as it takes. And remember the psalm: *The Lord is close to the brokenhearted.*"

During those days, I continued to stop into Our Lady of Perpetual Help after work. I'd sit in a rear pew, soaking in the silence of the empty church. I wondered why I had survived, and where my life might go from here.

The wave of publicity about the arrests died down after a few weeks, but I continued to get interview requests, invitations to speak at journalism conferences, and a few job offers.

The call from the managing editor at the *Boston Globe* was still rattling around in my head. He said they had formed a dedicated investigative reporting unit and he wanted me on it.

"You're a rare bird, Meg," he said. "Not everyone is cut out for this kind of work."

Schramm's words, coming back around. I supposed that was true. I was able to do this kind of work. In the end, though, I passed on that offer and the others. Something felt unfinished in West Wicklow. If I left now, wouldn't it prove that I was just another ruthless, ambitious reporter, looking to make a name for myself and then moving on?

One of the things that bothered me about being pulled off the story was that I never got a chance to confront Ducharme. In the classic investigative reporting process, you doggedly assemble all of your evidence, records, statements by others and then, in the final step, you confront the person accused of wrongdoing and say, "what do you have to say for yourself? Why did you do these things?" This story took a different path. It made the leap from newspaper investigation to criminal arrests and that meant the lawyers did all the talking. Bob got some comments from Ducharme's attorney about how the charges were "baseless" and "driven by irresponsible, sensationalist reporting." His client, he maintained, would be completely vindicated.

The only insight into Ducharme's motives came in the profile story that Bob and Maddie put together after the arrest. Maddie found his high school yearbook in the library. West Wicklow High School Class of 1952. We all gathered around her desk to stare at his senior portrait.

His face had a look of confidence that was lacking in most of the black-and-white images around him. It was more than just confidence, I realized, the longer I studied him. His black hair fell into a roguish wave across his forehead, his head tilted, chin down, movie-star style. The faint hint of a smirk in the corner of the lips. A gaze of serene and almost bemused certainty. He was a superior being, and knew it.

The yearbook held few other clues. He appeared in none of the athletic team photos but was seated in the center of the Future Business Leaders of America club as its president. The only other trace of him was found on the page that chronicled the senior prom. He stood off to one side of the gymnasium, surrounded by a clutch of boys and girls who looked at him with rapt attention as he appeared to tell a story, gesturing broadly with both hands.

Maddie went through the senior class list, tracked down those who still lived in the area and managed to get interviews with a half-dozen. Bob worked his contacts throughout the town, talking to former employees, girlfriends and business partners. What emerged was a profile of a brash, driven and willful man who became increasingly isolated and secretive over the years.

After high school, he enrolled at Babson College in Wellesley, Massachusetts, a prestigious, private school focused on business education. A woman who dated him during those years said he confided to her once that his greatest fear was being poor.

"He said his mother and father had both worked in the mills as teenagers. She used to tell him stories about being hungry and having holes in the bottoms of their shoes. He said they both worked like dogs to build a business," she told Maddie. "But his mother died when Roland was in high school. Tuberculosis. After that his father became totally focused on accumulating more and more wealth. Because life could be heartless, he said, and you had to scratch and claw to hold onto what was yours."

One high school classmate who later worked in the Ducharme shoe factory with father and son described "a cut-throat environment where every corner that could be cut to make another buck was cut, and then cut again until it bled."

The "old man" rode his son relentlessly. "Watching them together, it was like he was sculpting Roland into the image of himself. 'Go back and negotiate a better deal with the suppliers,' he would tell him. 'And don't come back until you do!'"

A few people remembered that Roland had married, briefly, in his thirties, and a check of records at the Town Hall confirmed that. "She was lovely, from a good family, but not good enough to suit his father," said a female high school classmate. "So the way I heard it, his loving dad paid her off, sent her away." After that, Roland was sometimes seen at country club dinners or the occasional charity event with different women, always stunning, but never the same woman twice.

The local businessmen that Bob interviewed described Ducharme in his later years as single-minded and humorless. After his father died and Roland assumed control of the company, he took the family zeal for amassing wealth to a new level. "He was really only about making money," said one construction contractor who had built several of his apartment complexes. "That was it. Even when he socialized at the club, it was all business. He had no interests. He didn't watch TV. You couldn't strike up a conversation about the movie everyone was talking about, or sports or what was happening in Washington, D.C. Only business. Cut and dried. No chit-chat."

All together, they interviewed seventeen people who knew Roland Ducharme at different points in his life. Not a single one of them defended him. Not a soul said he couldn't possibly have done these things.

By the fall of 1978, most of the players in the conspiracy had pleaded no contest in exchange for lighter sentences. That included Moreno, Nunes, the four firemen accomplices, and another half-dozen town officials who were charged with accepting bribes to look the other way. The most prominent of these were Police Chief Recchia and Fire Chief Lambert. Together they had formed the impenetrable "roadblock" Pelletier referred to back in the hospital room.

The only one who insisted on going to trial was Ducharme. To this day, I believe he was convinced he could somehow buy his way out of it.

Bob covered the trial. Because I was, as people kept constantly reminding me, a victim and scheduled to testify, I was not permitted to even observe the trial in the gallery.

The only time I saw the inside of the courtroom was on the day in late September when I took the stand. A warm wave of Indian summer had blanketed Rhode Island, and the courtroom at the federal building in Providence was stifling. I spotted Bob seated in the packed gallery. A few other familiar faces. Pelletier, in the first row behind the prosecution team. Ruskin sitting with the *Times'* attorney. Francie and Lonnie. And Darlene, with Petey on her lap, giving me a nod of encouragement as I passed.

After they swore me in and I sat down, there was a moment as the prosecutor rose to his feet when I glanced over at the defense table. Ducharme sat there with his lawyers, his chair slightly behind theirs, as though he had just pushed back from the dinner table to relax and enjoy the conversation. His arms were folded, and his face bore that same expression from the yearbook. Serenely cocky.

I responded to the prosecutor's questions, which were all focused on the afternoon of the explosion. For an event so life-changing, the recitation of what happened sounded oddly matter-of-fact as I heard my own words come out. How Marty had led us there. The way the door rolled shut. Eric saving me.

Then Perreira, the defense lawyer, rose to cross-examine me. He was short and stocky with a receding jet black hairline. He strode to the front of the courtroom with a glower in his eyes. I stared back.

174

The prosecutors as well as the *Times'* lawyer had prepared me; no one could compel me to answer any questions revealing my sources.

"Miss Sullivan," he said, "when did you first zero in on Mr. Ducharme as a target of your..." He paused. "Shall we say, your investigation?" He coated the last word with a smear of sarcasm.

"I followed the facts where they led me."

He spun around.

"Facts? And who determines what is factual? You, I suppose?"

"Facts are facts. No one needs to determine them. Just find them."

The prosecutor rose to object. "Your honor, is there a point to this line of questioning?"

Perreira looked up at the judge. "I'm just about to get there, your honor."

"Continue," said the judge.

"Miss Sullivan, who appointed you to your investigatory position?"

"I was hired by Clive Ruskin, publisher of the *Arcadia Valley Daily Times*, to be a reporter."

"Oh, so it's just a job for hire? No special training in law enforcement or proper investigatory practices, and so on?"

"I have a degree in journalism, including courses in investigative reporting, media law..."

He interrupted me and turned to face the jury.

"Isn't it true, Miss Sullivan, that you landed in this town as a completely inexperienced and ambitious young reporter and that you set your sights on Mr. Ducharme because he was a prominent businessman who would make a sensational target?"

For a split second I remembered the war room wall with Ducharme's name nowhere to be found. Then all the tiny breadcrumbs that led me to him. Perreira was partially right in one respect. I did have a gut instinct about Ducharme before I had any real evidence. But my instinct was right.

"I came here to dig for the truth. Wherever it led. That's what I did."

In the end, the jury didn't buy Perreira's theory that a reckless reporter had triggered a witch hunt to smear an innocent man. Bob called the newsroom from a pay phone at the courthouse. Talked to Ned. Convicted on all charges.

175

Ned made the announcement to the staff and a cheer went up. Ruskin came out of his office, leading a slow, hard hand-clap that built into a mighty and defiant thunder. Maddie rushed over to my desk and wrapped her arms around me. Her eyes glistened and she looked embarrassed for a moment, then hugged me again. Over her shoulder, I could see Ned's grin lighting up the whole room.

That night, I went to Estrella's hoping to talk to Darlene. When she came over to take my order she slid into the booth next to me.

"I heard from Joan," she said in a whisper. "She's doing really good. New job, new town. She couldn't say where. But she told me to thank you."

"I'm glad things worked out for her," I said. I regretted not being able to see her testify. When I read Bob's account afterward, a fond sort of pride flowed through me. She sat composed and confident, speaking in a strong voice, for close to two hours during her testimony and cross-examination. She never glanced in Ducharme's direction on her way out, leaving it all behind her.

"And what about you?" Darlene asked. "Are you going to leave West Wicklow?"

Faces like hers made me almost want to stay. Honest and open and kind. But it was finally time to leave.

"I'm headed to Boston. To the *Globe*."

She squealed, causing heads to turn all around us. "That's a really big-deal paper! Good for you, Meg!"

I had called the editor back after I testified. I figured I would just try to stay on his radar. Maybe at some point there might be another opening.

"When can you start?" he asked. "I've got a hot one here. Possible Superfund toxic waste site brewing. I could really use the help."

I said my goodbyes to the newsroom gang at a going-away party at The Rock. Even Ruskin and Sandy Frazier stopped by for a few minutes to wish me well before Queen's thunderous *We Will Rock You* drove them out.

John shouted to me over the din.

"I'm telling you right now, you're not going to find stuffies this good in Boston."

Bob piped up. "And those Boston officials will be nothing compared to West Wicklow. You are going to be so, so bored."

Joel gave me a framed print of a photo he took of me at the Town Council meeting protest, perched in my seat, taking notes. In the background behind me was Eric, quieting the angry crowd. I didn't have a single photo of him. I started to fill up and Joel reached over to wrap me in a hug.

Maddie slid onto the stool next to me, her mouth scrunched into a pout.

"I'm losing my soul sister."

"It's up to you to keep the flame burning, you know," I said. "Girls can do this kind of work."

She raised her beer to clink mine.

"Damn right we can!"

Ned was the hardest goodbye.

"You know, Boston is only an hour away," I said.

"I think we'll be friends for a long, long time, Meg—at least I hope so. Besides, it's award season now. You know we're going to submit this story for all the big ones. We may meet again soon at one of those fancy banquets."

He paused for a moment, looking down.

"And if we do well, I may float the resume out there again."

"You would be a stellar addition to any newsroom," I said solemnly, the beer starting to make me a bit flowery in my language.

But I meant every word.

I had one more farewell that needed to be said. I hadn't stepped inside the police department headquarters in months, relegated to covering stories about zoning, public schools and anything I could dig up that wasn't crime-related. As I entered, Teddy looked puzzled.

"Here to see the chief," I said. "I have an appointment."

He looked down to check a sheet on his desk.

"Yes, you do," he said. He pointed up the staircase. "You know the way."

Upstairs, I found a doorway marked with a makeshift nameplate typed on white paper: *Armand Pelletier, Chief of Police.*

He rose from his desk to greet me with a warm handshake.

"I hear you're leaving us," he said. "West Wicklow's loss. And mine. I could use another pair of eyes, just to make sure we've cleaned out all the vermin."

"I expect no vermin are going to hang around now that you're in charge," I said.

In the wake of the arrests, the council had named Mrs. Boucher acting president, and she, in turn, appointed Pelletier acting chief. Once former chief Recchia's plea deal was finalized, the council named Pelletier to the permanent position.

"To put this nightmare behind us, West Wicklow needs a chief with absolute integrity and guts, and I believe we have found that person in Armand Pelletier," Boucher said at the meeting where the council unanimously approved his appointment.

Now, I sat across the desk from him and soaked in the view of Main Street rooftops in the window behind his head. How fitting. A perch from which he could keep an eye on things.

I asked how his officers had reacted when it was revealed at trial that he had helped the FBI nail the conspirators.

"Most of them were glad to see the whole mess cleaned up," he said. "We'd all spent many months walking on eggshells, not knowing exactly what game was being played. And the ones who didn't like what I did, well, they're no longer here."

A world-weary smile creased his face. "But that's history now, for both of us. You know, I have some buddies in the Boston P.D. Very solid operation up there. Let me know if I can ever help you."

"Are any of them skilled in the art of communicating anonymously with reporters via their mailbox?"

He raised his eyebrows.

"They would never, ever do such a thing. I believe they leave messages in flower pots."

The night before I left West Wicklow to drive to Boston an early-season storm dumped a foot of snow, the first sizeable accumulation since I'd moved there. Francie was ecstatic.

"I knew these would come in handy someday," she said, yanking her old Maine snowshoes off the side of the house and stomping around the driveway to help me load the Hornet. Lonnie came over in his four-wheel drive to shovel us out.

"From now on, I think I'll always try to rent this apartment to a reporter," she said as our parkas tried to compress into an awkward hug. "You guys definitely keep things interesting."

On my first week on the job at the *Globe*, the news came across the wire that Ducharme had been sentenced to the death penalty and would be sent to the federal high-security prison in Lewisburg,

Pennsylvania, while he pressed his appeal. On my second week on the job, the phone at my desk rang. It was Manuel Perreira.

"Mr. Ducharme would like to offer you the opportunity to interview him."

The word "speechless" was in my vocabulary but I had never actually experienced it until that moment.

"Miss Sullivan, are you there?"

When my voice finally returned I asked why.

"He has something he would like to discuss with you that he believes you will find of interest."

The drive to Lewisburg was five hours, giving me too much time to think about what lay ahead of me. I'd talked to my editor and he thought the interview could make a great first-person Sunday magazine piece. Maybe I was finally ready to write it.

On the way, I wondered if he planned to confess to me, to show remorse in a bid to avoid the death penalty. Maybe he'd offer to use his money to make reparation in some way.

None of those scenarios sounded like the Ducharme I had observed.

From a distance, the penitentiary resembled a college campus, commanding a wide-open site amid the frozen farmlands of central Pennsylvania, with a tall stone tower and buildings the color of cocoa clustered tightly together. A patchy crust of snow still covered the surrounding grounds from the earlier Nor'easter.

I showed my press credentials at the entrance and was buzzed inside. The guard at the command center in the narrow lobby dispatched an impossibly tall and beefy corrections officer to escort me. He walked next to me down a long hallway that was encased in hard surfaces and illuminated by a harsh, bright light. The clack of our footsteps bounced off the walls, making it sound as though there were others trailing behind us.

After a turn to the right, we sidestepped a lawyerly man in a suit with an overstuffed briefcase who was headed back toward the exit with another officer. An intense quiet blanketed the place, interrupted by the periodic rock-hard clang of a door and locks sliding into place.

My escort led me through one set of locked doors into a small waiting area, and then through another into a meeting room devoid of color or ornament. Perreira stood against one of the beige walls. He nodded almost imperceptibly.

The guard motioned for me to sit in one of two chairs positioned at a metal table in the center of the room. He posted next to the door, arms folded.

I waited. Three minutes. Four. Five.

Then, the unlocking noise.

Another officer led Ducharme in, handcuffed, and guided him into the other chair. The guard positioned himself at Ducharme's elbow—within grabbing distance. Reassuring.

I thought I had prepared myself for the emotions I would feel. That ball of anger remained inside me but I had learned to manage it, I thought. Now I felt it tightening again.

The last time I'd been this close to him was the day I tried to ambush him at his office. Close enough to smell his cologne. None of that in the air today. Yet, even in his orange garb, he looked like a man who still believed he had a card or two left to play. A man with an agenda.

"It's been a while since we last spoke, Meg."

I winced at his use of my first name.

I leaned toward him.

"Did you ask for this interview so you could confess?"

He burst into a laugh so oddly loud it made the two officers stiffen.

"You reporters," he said, wagging a finger at me, "always jumping to false conclusions. To the contrary, I want to assert my innocence."

"You did none of those things you were convicted for?"

"Not a one. I am the victim here. The victim of a callous witch hunt by you and your little paper, as well as a betrayal by greedy business associates. I have no doubt that I will be vindicated."

I continued to write furiously to capture his words while trying to control my urge to stick my pen in one of his cold blue eyes.

"You see," he continued, "if others committed certain acts because they thought those things might please me, that they would somehow earn my favor, well, that is certainly not my fault. But I do have a very interesting opportunity for you. A chance for you to clear your name. Clear your conscience."

It was at that point that I began to wonder for the first time if Roland Ducharme was in full possession of his faculties. Or was it possible for a sane human being to achieve this magnitude of evil?

His tone shifted slightly and I got the sense that he was viewing this as a business negotiation.

"Meg, I'm sure you're aware that there are many innocent people, wrongly accused, rotting away in facilities like this. And some very honorable journalists have taken up their cause, launching investigations into the investigation, as it were. Trying to expose the true perpetrators.

"Imagine if you and I wrote a book together. A co-authored book that really digs deep into the evidence and posits a new theory: that Roland Ducharme was wrongly targeted and then framed."

I'd had enough of this monologue.

"Who exactly do you think framed you?"

He leaned back in his chair. "That's for us to flesh out in writing the book. Meg, I know you are ambitious. What could bring you greater notoriety than this? It would be a blockbuster!"

He paused. "And, of course, someone providing this kind of ghostwriting service would earn a handsome fee. Despite all of the government seizures and such, I still have tremendous resources, you know. Some writers earn as much as seven figures for this kind of project."

I snapped my notebook shut.

"I decline." I looked over at my escort. "I'm finished."

He led me out first. I couldn't resist glancing back one last time. He sat there with that same yearbook expression on his face. Still certain that somehow, he would beat this.

Chapter Nineteen

Ned was right. We did see each other again on the banquet circuit that spring. Several times. The mill fire investigation was honored with awards from the New England Press Association, UPI, and, the granddaddy of all, a Pulitzer for Public Service.

"See?" I whispered to Ned on the stage as photographers snapped away. "You weren't just a one-Pulitzer wonder after all."

"Remember my cautionary tale," he murmured back. "Watch your liquor!"

The awards generated more requests for me to speak at other events, but I turned all of them down except for one. I was still more of a writer than a talker. But when the offer came to speak to the graduating journalism majors at Oakmont, I knew I had some things I wanted to tell them.

The spring timing was fortunate. On that same trip I was able to serve as maid of honor for Eveline as she exchanged wedding vows with Dad in a tiny chapel in Cape May. In the pocket of her cream-colored suit, she carried something borrowed.

"This helped keep me going and brought me luck," I said to her just before the ceremony, pressing the Cape May diamond into her hand.

"I'll be its caretaker for now," she whispered. "But if you ever need it again, you know where to find it."

At a small reception hosted by the nuns at the Wedding Cake, Dad and I danced to an old Dean Martin song on a reel-to-reel tape system someone had donated to the order long ago.

"I'm happy for your success but wish you were a little closer than Boston," he fretted. "The *Washington Post* would be only a stone's throw away from Philly, you know."

I shook my head. "I think New England's gotten into my blood. There's something stoic about it that appeals to me."

A few days after the wedding, I drove the familiar route through the tree-lined streets of West Philadelphia to the Oakmont campus. It was early afternoon and sunlight streamed through the newborn maple leaves, painting the stone and brick buildings with splashes of fluorescent green. I remembered the four springs I had spent there— the best of all seasons. The smell of honeysuckle in the air. Throwing Frisbees on the lawn of the Quad until we had to slink sheepishly into class late.

It was mid-afternoon, a few hours before I was scheduled to give my talk. I wanted to spend some time walking around campus. I parked near my old dorm, and passed the spot where I'd interviewed John Harrington. The young maple in the sidewalk had grown a bit, its trunk a little sturdier. I'd thought about John many times during my stay in West Wicklow. I still carried the wrinkled slip of paper with his sister's number in my wallet, thinking that I would call her sometime.

I saw the student union building up ahead and slipped into the stream of students climbing the stairs to go inside. I would have a cup of coffee in the lounge, one of my old favorite hangouts. Along the right side of the lobby, I passed the familiar bank of pay phones with their mahogany privacy panels enclosing each, students hunched over, receivers cradled against their ears. The phone at the end was open. *Why not now?* I dug a few quarters out of the bottom of my purse and pulled the scrap of paper from my wallet.

His sister answered. I introduced myself.

"I hope I'm not disturbing you. I just wanted to see how John was doing."

A long pause.

Finally she spoke. "I'm afraid things didn't turn out quite the way I hoped."

She said John had seemed to adjust well at first, living with her and her family.

"My husband was trying to help him get a job. John put in an application at the Post Office but got turned down because of an old arrest for disorderly conduct during his days on the street.

"A little while after that, he told me he needed to leave. Something about feeling confined. He told me he loved me. I made him promise to call every week so I would know he's safe and okay."

It was as if something precious on a particular shelf in my memory had been knocked to the ground without warning, breaking into a hundred jagged pieces. "Where is he now?"

"He let us buy him a bus ticket to Miami and then he worked his way down to the Keys. He has a place to stay, picks up some odd jobs. He says he's happier there."

I didn't know what to say. I had hoped for a different ending, but maybe this was a better one in his eyes.

"I hope you don't feel bad," she said. "For me, getting back in touch with him was a gift. He's still in my life, even now."

"The next time he calls, would you tell him I was asking for him?" I said.

"I will. He'll be glad to hear you called. John told me many times that you talking to him on that sidewalk was the best thing that ever happened to him. He called it a miracle."

Later, I stood on the stage of Oakmont's auditorium and looked out at faces so young and innocent. Is that how I looked when I landed in West Wicklow? It seemed like decades had passed. I felt the wave of nerves that always came when I had to speak, but I willed it away. This was too important to mess up.

I told them about the things I had experienced and the things I had learned. I described the harrowing times and the times I almost gave up. But even more than all of that, I wanted them to understand what they were signing up for.

"To do this work, you have to accept the hard truth that human beings are capable of things more shameful than you've ever imagined. And yet you somehow have to maintain your faith that there are more good people than bad, and that there will be good people who stand up and help you dig out the truth.

"Hold onto your idealism. Don't be discouraged when, despite your best efforts, your story doesn't accomplish what you hoped. Don't give in to cynicism. In a lot of communities large and small across this country, you may be the only one standing in the way of someone bent on hurting people. The public counts on us. Even when they don't like us. Even when they call us biased. When they call us liars. Or say that we're only in it to sell papers.

"Don't expect the public to throw bouquets at you. The only applause you're likely to get is from your own peers. And that's fine. We don't need people to like us. But we do need to play the role that only we can play. To comfort the afflicted and afflict the comfortable. To dig, and keep digging until every truth is uncovered."

When I finished speaking, there was a half-second of absolute silence and then a young man in the second row jumped to his feet, raised his fist in the air and shouted, "Hell, yeah!" Suddenly everyone was standing, roaring, stomping their feet. If I hadn't been so utterly embarrassed, hoping to disappear into a hole under the stage, I might have considered this moment one of the high points of my life.

In the back of the room, Mr. Schramm stood, clapping along with the other journalism professors. Afterward, he approached me.

"You've done well, Meg," he said, shaking my hand. The raspy voice was the same, but the way he looked at me was different. Not the same skeptical face that had glowered down at me, challenging me. "I have to be honest," he continued. "You surprised the hell out of me. I misjudged you by a mile. Didn't see the toughness in you."

"Don't feel bad. I didn't see it either."

When spring came in earnest to New England in the waning days of May, I steered the Hornet toward Boston's South Shore, scouting for a new apartment that might be close to, or even have a glimpse of, the water. I followed my map from one quaint town to another, my window rolled down. The first warm spring days in this part of the world, I'd learned, felt almost like a miracle. A healing balm on chapped skin. A giddy reward for the extra weeks of chill and grey.

I pushed a cassette into the player I'd placed on the passenger seat. It was a mix tape Eric had made for me. It started with *Be My Baby* and included some of the other music from those brief months. The track playing now was *Three Little Birds* from reggae master Bob Marley's latest album, a favorite Eric used to play in his Jeep. We would sing along with the comforting lyrics: *every little thing gonna be alright...* I dialed up the volume and let the rhythm carry me on a gentle wave.

I crossed a low bridge over an inlet from Weymouth into Hingham, a village teetering on the edge of a series of harbors and bays that stretched up to Boston. I followed the map to the address of an apartment I'd seen listed in the *Globe* classifieds. As I turned left onto Shipyard Drive, I entered a district that lived up to its name: clearly a working waterfront with tall, weathered barn-like structures and docks full of commercial fishing boats.

I found my way to number 21. The sign said Vanderweld & MacKay Yacht Builders. I double-checked the address in the paper. Yes, 21. This had to be it.

"The apartment's upstairs, over the sail loft," said the young man with winter-tanned skin at the counter. "I can show you."

I followed him up a wooden staircase.

"You a sailor?" he called back over his shoulder.

"I hope to be. With some practice."

He opened the door to a tiny apartment with large windows overlooking Hingham Harbor. It was painted a weathered blue and smelled of cedar and salt.

"I'll take it."

As we handled the lease paperwork, he asked if I was in the market for a boat.

"Yes, a small one," I said.

"We just took a daysailer in trade for a larger boat. If you're interested, you could keep it here on our dock. A little easier than trailering a boat for..."

He paused, looking flustered. I supposed he was going to say "for a woman." In fairness, I didn't much look like an old salt.

"Let's see her," I said.

We walked along a narrow dock that hugged the building and entered the boatyard.

"Here she is. Little beauty."

Up on a wooden rack was a sleek boat, similar to Eric's but with a mast that towered high above us. I peered up to the top of it, shielding my eyes from the warming sun.

"She's got a 20-foot mast. Little bit of a high-aspect ratio for a daysailer, so she'll be fast. She'll test you."

I didn't know what "high-aspect ratio" meant, but a fast boat sounded like a good one to learn on. For $385, she was mine. It was the most I'd ever paid for something with my own money. I christened her *Muckraker*.

On the first fair Saturday after I moved in, the yard launched her and left her tied up and waiting for me in her small spot on the dinghy dock. I set off with a life preserver, a crisp new chart and a book called *Let's Learn to Sail* that I'd read cover to cover, twice. And also a canoe paddle, strongly recommended by the guy at the ship's store.

"The wind does die sometimes out there, you know," he said with concern.

Actually, I didn't know. But I would learn.

I raised the main and pushed off the dock. So many sweet echoes of that earlier sparkling day. Sharing control with the wind. Memories I could let myself replay now.

As the wind filled the sail, I felt for the first time how open the waters were in front of me. I started out on a run, but as I reached the entrance to Hingham Bay I turned onto a fine broad reach and unfurled the jib.

She was quick and sure-footed. I felt no trace of fear.

ABOUT THE AUTHOR

Lu Anne Stewart has been writing professionally for more than 30 years in many different roles: newspaper reporter, editor, communications consultant and storyteller. After earning a bachelor's degree in English from the University of Pennsylvania and a master's in journalism from Columbia University, she went on to spend seven years as a reporter and editor for newspapers in Pennsylvania and Rhode Island. Since that time, she has enjoyed a long career as a corporate writer while always pursuing her passion for fiction-writing. She lives in Tampa, Florida, with her husband, Richard, and their feisty Chihuahua, Bella. Digging is her first novel.